For more than forty years,
Yearling has been the leading name
in classic and award-winning literature
for young readers.

Yearling books feature children's
favorite authors and characters,
providing dynamic stories of adventure,
humor, history, mystery, and fantasy.

Trust Yearling paperbacks to entertain,
inspire, and promote the love of reading
in all children.

# PATRICIA REILLY GIFF

maggie's
door

A Yearling Book

Visit us on the Web! www.randomhouse.com/kids

Educators and librarians, for a variety of teaching tools, visit us at
www.randomhouse.com/teachers

ISBN: 978-0-440-41581-7

Reprinted by arrangement with Wendy Lamb Books

Printed in the United States of America

January 2008

13 12 11 10 9 8 7 6 5 4

TO HAROLD REILLY,
WITH LOVE

# GLOSSARY

| | | |
|---|---|---|
| *a stór* | uh **stoar** | my dear |
| *bean sídhe* | ban-**shee** | female fairy beings who wail when someone is about to die |
| *Dia dhuit* | **djee**-a **ditch** | God save you (a greeting) |
| *fuafar* | **fu**-uh-fur | disgusting, hateful |
| *ocras* | **ok**-rus | hunger |

# THE PEOPLE OF MAIDIN BAY

## THE RYAN FAMILY

---

Granda
Da
Maggie
Celia
Nory
Patch

## THE MALLON FAMILY

---

Mrs. Mallon
Mary
Francis
Michael
Liam
Sean

## THEIR NEIGHBOR

---

Anna Donnelly

THE HUNGER

A terrible stench drifted over the land. The potato crop had failed. For the families who lived in Maidin Bay it meant that nothing but a little fish, seaweed, or a few leaves boiled in water was left for them to eat.

They had to leave or starve. One by one they took the road to Galway. Ships waited there, ships that might take them across the sea to America.

Nory Ryan was the last of her family to go. . . .

LEAVING

# ONE

## NORY

Nory hadn't gone far, just over the rise, when she heard it.

A voice?

*"Ocras,"* it screamed. *"Ocras."*

*Hunger.*

Nory took another step and stopped. On one side of her were the dunes, on the other the great ocean. A strange place she was in, with wisps of fog drifting across the road. And again that sound.

The wind, she told herself, even though she knew it wasn't.

Granda had told her of selkies, half seal, half human. When they lived on land they wept bitter tears for the deep; when they returned to the sea they mourned for lost loves on the land.

Was that it? The cry of some poor selkie woman? Such an eerie sound.

The crying stopped and Nory began to walk again. One foot in front of the other. Away from home, away from that empty house with the door banging in the wind. The trip just beginning.

The sand drifted across the road, grains of it sticking to her bare feet. The crying reminded her of her little brother, Patch, and the last time she had seen him, his arms flung out to her from the back of her friend Sean Red Mallon's cart.

And where was that cart now, Sean pulling its heavy weight while Patch leaned against Mrs. Mallon in back? How far had they gone along that winding road toward the port of Galway?

She quickened her steps.

*Don't think about Patch, or the Mallons, or the rest of the family, all gone ahead to find a ship,* she told herself. *Just keep going. Nearly at the crossroads.*

"*Ocras, ocras,*" came the cry again, and with it the sound of powerful wings.

That was what it was, then, not a voice but the call of a great seabird.

It swooped down over her head, too close. She dropped her bag and clutched the top of her head with both hands. As the bird rose she saw the snow-white body, the huge wingspan, the curved beak, and eyes that were strangely human.

She had seen such a bird once when she and Granda had walked along the cliff ledge. Granda had thrown it a piece of dulse from his pocket. "Travelers must give the white bird food. It will bring luck until the end of the journey," he had told her.

"But we're only going home," she had said. "Only a few steps."

"Ah, still."

Granda. How she missed him!

But what could she give the bird?

She had so little—papers Da had sent that would get her onto a ship, and a coin from her neighbor Anna sewed into her shawl, and what was in her bag, the bits of things Anna had managed to put together for the long trip ahead of her: herbs for illness, a biscuit so hard it had to be soaked in water, a bit of meat, and two pieces of brack, rock hard as the biscuit.

The bird circled over her, higher now. Nory dropped to the ground, scrambling for the bag, and reached deep inside for the biscuit. Anna's voice was in her ear: *"There are only these bits of food between you and starvation. Guard them."*

She held the biscuit in her hand as the bird wheeled over her head once more, but it was too hard to break into pieces. Suppose she threw all of it?

*Between you and starvation,* the wind said.

*"Traveler's luck,"* Granda whispered in her head.

What should she do? Her mouth tingled with the thought of that biscuit, the softness of it when she'd find a stream for dipping, the taste of it on her tongue.

There was no time to think or the bird would be gone.

She took a step forward, reached over her head, and tossed the biscuit high into the air.

Effortlessly the bird swooped to catch it in its beak. It climbed high over the dunes with it and headed out over the waves that broke at the edge of the strand.

"It's the whole biscuit," she called. "For my whole family. Remember that." Her hair blew into her face and she raked it back impatiently so she could see where the bird went. "We're all of us traveling."

And that voice in her head again: *But you, Nory, are alone.*

The bird skimmed over the surf, but then, just before it was out of sight, it dropped the biscuit into the sea.

Nory's hand went to her mouth, hard against her teeth. *Foolish girl,* Anna would have said. *You needed that food to stay alive.*

Nory cupped her hands around her mouth. "Don't forget us. All of us. Da. Granda and Celia. Patch . . . and my friend Sean Red Mallon. Don't forget Sean."

The bird was almost out of sight. "We are trying for America," she called after it. "We want to stand at Maggie's door in Brooklyn."

## TWO

NORY

Up ahead was the crossroad. What had Da said? *"The road to the ships winds around like a ball of yarn let loose. Just stay on that road."*

It was the one to the right, the one that hugged the sea all the way to the port of Galway. Every year Da had taken it to find a fishing boat. But the other road, the small winding muddy boreen, led only to Patrick's Well, up and up, and the well almost hanging off the edge of the cliff.

How could she leave without one last look?

She had been to the well a day ago to say goodbye. But this was forever. She'd never be back. She'd never see it again, not any of it.

She stood there hesitating, then shrugged off the bag she carried over her shoulder. Tucking it into the high grass where no one could see it, she went past the small cemetery where Mam had lain since the week Patch was born, and up to the well, where she could look back and see her house. There the wind blew itself fiercely across the wide stone flags, and far below, the sea spread itself out like a great gray plate against a pewter sky.

Above her head the tree branches rattled in the wind. She closed her eyes and it seemed she could see the faces of all her family:

Da, deep lines around his eyes, squinting as he waved goodbye on his way to fish last year.

Months later Granda and her sister Celia leaving their small house desperate to find Da, to tell him the potatoes had failed.

And Patch. Back to Patch again. Only a few days ago she had put him on Sean Red Mallon's cart. "You must go," she had said as he tried to hold on to her. "You must have that chance."

How strange it was. A year ago it had been only her big sister Maggie who was going across the sea to America with her new husband, Sean's brother Francey. Now the whole family was going, one by one, trying to escape the hunger that gnawed at their stomachs and even their bones.

Nory opened her eyes, remembering the bonfire they had lighted the night of Maggie's wedding a year ago. Great flames had leapt up against the sky, sending shadows against the stones of their house.

"Dance with me again, Nory," her friend Sean Red Mallon had said, his red hair as bright as the bonfire, his hand out to her.

"Do you think you're the only one I'll dance with

this night?" Her feet had tapped to the sound of the fiddle.

Sean had leaned forward, laughing. "Then you'll have to dance with your granda, and I'm better at it than he is."

Better than Granda perhaps, but still Granda, tall and thin and white-bearded, had danced the night through, danced with Maggie, who wore Mam's wedding dress, danced with Nory's second sister, Celia, danced holding little Patch on his shoulders.

And Maggie, glowing, happy: "Don't be sad, Nory. Da will come home from his great fishing trip. And sometime you'll all join me at 416 Smith Street, Brooklyn, America."

"It will be years," Nory had said. "It will be forever until then."

The wind howled around Nory now, and birds screeched as they flew over the well and out to the sea. But not the great bird with her biscuit.

Nory sank down on the rough wall, and it seemed that a terrible smell rose up around her, though it had been carried off months ago by the wind.

The smell that had changed their lives forever.

The potatoes.

She turned to look back over the fields that curved down to the sea, fields that in some winters were covered with a thin blanket of snow, and in the growing season a riot of purple potato blossoms.

But not last year.

Not this year.

The blight had turned those potatoes to mush, to ooze, leaving everyone hungry. Starving.

Still now over Patrick's Well hung bits of cloth, prayers that people had left. There was one of her sister Celia's shifts.

*Ah, Celia with the turned-up nose.*

"I will stay alive," Celia had said when she and Granda left, her dress huge on her bones. "Granda and I will get to the ships. We will find Da and send for you and Patch. Together we will get to Maggie's door in America."

Another sound now.

The fall of a rock behind her. Not a bird this time. She spun around. "Anna!"

Anna Donnelly, her neighbor. Anna, who had taught her about cures and healing, and who had taken her in with Patch when everyone else had gone.

Anna stood there in her white cap, her skirt ruffling in the wind, her face as wrinkled as the potatoes had been. She put her hands on her hips, angry. "What are you doing here, Nory Ryan?"

Nory slid off the edge of the well. "A last look."

Anna's eyes were fierce. "And where is your bag?"

"In the sea grass below. Safe," Nory said, glad that Anna didn't know about the biscuit.

"You are wasting time," Anna said. "You must go now and never look back. Take that road."

Nory looked down where Anna pointed, at the same road that Da and Granda and Celia had taken, that Patch and the Mallons were following.

*Patch, her little brother, stick-thin legs dangling from the back of the cart, fine pale hair flattened to his head by the spring squalls that spat across the road.*

8

"How can I leave you, Anna? You have been so good to me." Nory reached out to her. "How can I go alone?"

"I belong here." Anna's mouth was a thin line. "But you must save yourself."

For one quick moment Nory held Anna to her before she went back down the boreen to reach for her bag and sling it over her shoulder.

It was only a moment to the crossroad.

"I'm going to find them, all the people I love," she called to the wind as she turned, and to the bird that had long disappeared. In her mind suddenly was a picture of Sean Red Mallon, her friend since they were younger than Patch. She thought of Sean's blazing red hair, and his height, and the way he smiled when he looked down at her.

*"Dance with me, Nory."*

What would Sean say if he knew she was just days behind them?

She began to hurry.

THE ROAD

# THREE

## SEAN

Almost there.

Sean Red Mallon pulled the cart slowly, the wheels grinding over the stones. As the road turned away from the sea and back again, the things they had taken with them—Da's stool, one of the great hooks that his brothers Liam and Michael used for fishing, Francey's boots—slid back and forth. His mam and little Patch leaned one way and then another.

How long could he pull that cart without food? The road shimmered in front of him, almost fading away, and he had to blink to find it again.

"Sean," Patch called. "Do you have a bit of dulse in your pocket? Just a wee bit of the seaweed?"

Sean shook his head, even though Patch faced the back of the cart and couldn't see him.

"You know there's no dulse," Mam said. Her voice

was rough, as always, and Sean felt sorry for the boy. How old was he? Four maybe?

"Nory always brought me dulse," Patch said, "brought it right out of the sea."

"There's no hint of it out there today . . . ," Sean began, and stopped. It was too much effort to say that they didn't even have the strength to wade in and drag the seaweed out. Too much effort to say that if the smear of purple appeared along the water's edge, people lying along the strand or at the edge of the road would scoop it up long before he could get to it.

Sean took his hands off the cart posts. Long ago when he was Patch's age, they had had a donkey to pull the cart. It was a small irritable animal with thick yellow teeth who turned to nip at them once in a while. Sean's older brother Francey would jump back, scooping Sean up in his arms away from the donkey's mouth just in time, laughing. But no wonder the donkey had been irritable. He'd tell that to Francey when they reached Brooklyn. He tried to grin but the skin around his mouth was loose and didn't even move.

He stopped then, dreaming about the times when there had been potatoes growing strong in the fields and they'd had enough to fill their stomachs. He brushed away the memory of the potatoes failing, the plants sinking into a mess of ooze, everyone starving.

Sean unwrapped the bits of cloth around his fingers and looked down at his hands. They were purple with bruises and raw with blisters that had broken. Something was wrong with his wrist as well . . . not only from pulling the cart but from the fight the second night they were on the road.

14

"A great cart," someone had said, and two boys had come around in front to try to take it from them. They were small and thin and no match for him even though he had never fought before, just mock fights with his brother Francey, wrestling on the earthen floor of the house or on the gritty sand below the cliffs.

Sean had pulled the cart away at last, leaving both boys gasping at the side of the road. Since then he had watched, barely sleeping at night, barely stopping during the day, so afraid that someone bigger, stronger, might come along and take the cart from him. Without it, Mam and Patch would never make the port.

Patch was whimpering. "I want Nory. I want my sister." Sean closed his eyes. He wanted Nory there. He could see her climbing the cliffs as she had done last winter for food.

"Go on now," Mam said. "The road is long."

Sean wrapped the rags around his hands again and reached for the cart posts. Ahead of him the road took a steep drop. How could he hold the cart against it?

He could see it in his mind, the road beginning its slide, the cart behind him, his hands backing along the posts as he tried to stop it. The front of the cart would push up against him, rolling faster. The wheels would tilt, his legs caught, his toes crushed.

His thoughts were so terrible that he hardly heard the sound of the man's feet moving along next to him, and when he did it was too late to get out of the way.

"Paddy," the voice called out to him.

Sean looked up, squinting, the sand in his eyes. An English gentleman like Lord Cunningham back in

Ballilee. His boots were high-shined even though mud had come up to spatter them here and there.

Sean's mouth went dry. "Yes, your honor, sir," he said.

"Stop the cart." The man spoke in English, the words sounding strange. He glanced down at his boots, irritated, and flicked at them lightly with the small whip he held in his hand.

Francey always said that Englishmen and trouble belonged together, and that was why Father Harte had taught the people in his parish many of their words. "It is good to know as much as you can," the priest had said. "To be prepared."

"I didn't steal the cart, sir," Sean told the man. "It is ours."

"My house is over the hill," the man said. "My horse went lame a mile back. Ask the groom to send me another."

Sean opened his mouth. "I can't leave the cart, sir," he said, but said it softly. "Someone will surely take it."

"I have no time to waste." The man's face was coarse, the teeth almost like their old donkey's. But Francey wouldn't have laughed at this donkey; he would have been angry.

"It won't take you long," the Englishman said. "Once you're up there, the cook will give you food."

Sean saw the man's eyes gleam, certain that he would do as he wished. Over his shoulder, Sean could see Mam's eyes were closed, sunken in her head.

"Food," Patch breathed.

There would be food on the long table in the man's great kitchen: a leg of lamb maybe, a chicken simmering in broth in the pot swung over the hearth. Eggs in a basket.

Eggs!

He took a breath. "Just over the hill?"

The man pointed with the crop. "And up the next a way." He shrugged. "It is simple. The groom will come back with the horse, and you will have food for your family."

"Sean, do it, *a stór*," his mother said without opening her eyes.

"Well, then . . . ," Sean said.

"An egg," Patch said, almost as if he knew Sean's thoughts.

Sean ran his hands over the knobby edges of the posts.

Without the cart they would never get to the port of Galway. But without something to eat . . .

"Sean," his mother said.

The day was almost over. It would be dark by the time he came back. It was a mistake.

"We need the food," his mother said.

He nodded at the man, not quite daring to look up at him. He'd do it.

## FOUR

### NORY

She passed a town and glanced at a stone church on a hill, its spires gray against the sky. Someday Patch would build houses and even a church like that, she was sure of it.

Patch loved to lie on the ground at the side of their house, a meandering line of stones in front of his out-spread arms. He'd rearrange the stones, adding to them, piling one upon another.

"Are you building a great city then?" she had asked him once.

"It is a house for you," he'd said, "with a room where you will sing and do nothing but that."

"That is a wonderful thing for you to do for me."

At first Nory did sing as she walked, bits of song she had made up. But the nights were different. Weird shapes rose in front of her and faded away as she came close to them.

*Only rocks or trees!* she told herself.

But suppose they were creatures who waited to spring out and twist themselves into the length of her hair, which fell to her waist?

She longed for the sound of Anna's voice, or Granda's. She knew what they'd say: *Never mind the fear. Make your way to the ship. There is no food left for you in Ireland.*

And now it was not only the nights that frightened her. The days were fearful as well. She didn't even know when the fear had begun.

She looked up to realize the road had separated and she was skirting a foamy finger of water. She stopped and followed her footsteps back a long way.

Suppose she went home to Maidin Bay? Over the last rise she would see Anna's wee house with plants growing from the thatched roof. Threads of smoke would rise from the hearth, and Anna would hold out her arms. Nory shook her head hard, feeling her hair whip around her. Anna would be furious.

"No more," Nory said aloud. She clenched her hands together. After a moment she began to sing again. She walked south.

Always south.

She kept the sea on her right side and tried to forget she was alone, that Anna was farther away with each step she took and the ship no nearer than the sliver of moon that slipped in between the clouds at night.

Sometimes people passed her on the road, people in tatters of clothing, holding out their hands for food, then disappearing in back of her.

But she wasn't afraid of those people. It was some-one else, someone who was following her. She could hear the footsteps soft on the packed earth of the road, and when she stopped, the steps stopped too.

"Ah, Nory," she told herself, but now she whispered. "It's only the crashing of the waves and the wind across the dunes."

She walked faster, panting as she climbed the next hill, then hesitated, trying to decide if she should look back over her shoulder and see . . .

See what? Nothing? Something from another world? She held her skirt up above her ankles and slid down the other side of the hill, gathering speed, too fast, much too fast.

She tried to slow down, reaching out to grab the chunks of sea grass in her hands. Just as she reached the bottom, her bag sliding away, something sharp sliced across the sole of her foot.

She sank down in the weeds at the side of the road, rocking back and forth, watching the blood blot itself in the sand underneath. With one hand she pulled the bag close. Wrapped in bits of cloth inside it were dried stems and leaves and flower petals. Anna's cures. *Houseleek for the eyes, laurel leaves for skin rash.* But nothing to stop the bleeding! Had she been home she could have covered the cut with a bit of fur from a hare.

Stomach heaving, head fuzzy, she thought of it dream-ily. Not a hare left in all of Ireland. Since the potato crop had failed, there were few creatures that hadn't been pounced on for food.

Somehow the bleeding had to be stopped. What it

needed was a stitch with a curved wire and a length of yarn, but she had neither.

She could see Anna's face. *Do you remember nothing I've taught you?*

*The web of a spider to cover a wound.*

She shuddered. Instead of looking for a web she pulled her skirt to her knees and used her teeth to tear it. The hem was so caked with mud it was as hard as the stones underneath her. She spat it out, tasting the grime of the road.

There was no help for it. It had to be a spider's web, and that spider had to be large enough to have spun a great amount of thread across the grasses. When she looked closely she could see dozens of small insects going busily about their world, climbing the rushes or burrowing along small ridges of sand. Small spiders the color of tea swung themselves across the tops of the reeds. And then she saw the right one: coal black, thick and hairy, with a web it had spun back and forth in the dry grass.

*Fuafar!*

She waved her hands, willing the spider to go away. She thought about killing it with a stone, but she could almost see Granda's face in front of her. *What kind of a thing is that, Nory,* he would say, *to take its web and its miserable life too?*

She leaned over and blew until at last the spider scuttled away from the windstorm she had created. She raised her foot, stepped on the web, and patted down its gauzy surface so it would cover the cut.

*Brave girl,* her sister Celia would say.

The sea was just beyond a small rise. On one foot she

hobbled off the road to reach the strand, then sank down in the damp sand. The water was clean and clear, icy cold, and she washed the hem of her skirt until it turned as blue as it had been the day last year when she had dyed the cloth with flowers from the field.

She tore off a long strip of the skirt to wind it around her foot, pulling the cloth tight. The blue turned pink almost immediately, but it was finished. She moved away from the sea, curled herself into a ball on the sand, and slept.

It was entirely dark when she opened her eyes again. She couldn't see the road in back of her, and just a glint of silver from the sea in front.

She was thirsty and cold, and her foot throbbed. Her neck prickled.

Alone, but not alone.

She twisted her head around slowly, and as her eyes became used to the darkness she saw the shape of the land. She caught her breath. A person, back bent, head up, was watching her from the top of the hill.

## FIVE

SEAN

It was late, and still the Englishman's house was not in sight. The moon was up and fast, rushing through clouds, lighting the fields around a small house.

The house listed on the edge of the road, almost as if it would slide away in the wind. Both halves of the door were shut tight or Sean would have stopped to ask if they knew how far he'd have to go to find the great house.

He paused to rest, but only for a moment before he went on. Running was easy for him. Francey had taught him to run lightly, and he had always been able to go on for long distances without becoming breathless.

Ah, Francey. At the end of this trip was Francey's house in Brooklyn. He pictured Francey and Maggie, his wife, and beside them his sister, Mary, who had gone to America first, so long ago he had just come up to her waist. He remembered Mary bent over him crying as she hugged him one last time, her cheeks lightly marked by the pits from smallpox.

At last around the bend he saw the walls and the iron gates, still open. He slipped in between them and went to the gatehouse.

"What is it?" The guard came outside, an iron pipe in his hand.

"Your master is on the road back there." Sean pointed. "He has need of a horse."

The man laughed without humor. "Do you think we'd give you a horse?"

Sean shook his head. "He asked that the groomsman bring him one."

The guard waved his hand. "We'll send one then. Go on."

Sean ran his tongue over his lips. They were dry, with the faintest taste of salt from the sea. "His honor said . . ."

The man turned his back and shuffled to the gates, hefting the pipe in his hand.

Sean spoke more loudly. "He said that I could have food."

"He never gives food. Never once in all the Hunger have I seen it."

"And for my family," Sean said. "My mam and a boy."

"Take yourself out through the gates." The man glanced at the pipe in his hand. "I have no time for you. I have to find the groomsman."

The path to the great house was long. The kitchen would be around the back. "His honor promised," Sean said.

The man's mouth twisted. "He gives nothing away."

Sean thought of eggs in a basket, a joint of meat on the table. He began to run. Ahead of him were trees and low bushes. If he could just get there, just hide . . .

He was faster than the guard, younger. He slipped behind a tree, motionless. He could hear the guard's footsteps, his heavy breathing. And then at last the guard said something under his breath and threw the pipe, which clanged against the gravel path.

Sean waited precious moments, then went around the corner of the great house to the kitchen. Everything there was dark and closed. He peered through the cracks in the door, trying to see if the fire was high or quiet and banked for the night. Would the guard go to the groomsman first or come to the kitchen?

"*Dia dhuit,*" he whispered, his mouth close to the door. He took a chance and pulled on the doorstrap.

The door opened and the face of a woman peered out, a heavy face with black currant eyes almost hidden in her nightcap. She ate every day, Sean thought, ate well from the Englishman's larder.

"Who is it?" The sound of Galway was thick on her tongue.

"You are the cook?" He looked over his shoulder, his heart pounding, his mouth dry. "His honor said to come for food. I helped him on the road."

She opened the door farther for him, and he went inside to see that she had been sleeping. Her straw bed was rumpled with coats piled on top of one another, and only the edges of the turf gleamed red in the darkness.

The room was as he had pictured it: the table, the

pot swung over the hearth, even the eggs in the wicker basket.

"What is it you want?" she asked.

There was enough food here to feed dozens of people on the road. He spread his hands wide. "What will you give me?"

"An egg?" she said.

He pictured it, cracking the top lightly, sucking the warm liquid. Gone in a moment. Nothing for Mam and Patch.

"More than an egg." He hesitated. "There are three of us."

She went back to her bed, pattering on feet too small for her bulk. "Take what you can carry," she said. "No one will know the difference."

It was hard to believe his luck. He stopped to crack an egg and, with his head held back, let the inside spill over his tongue. A hen's egg! He ate another and another.

He filled his pockets with two others. He wanted to ask if he could take the wicker basket, but already the woman was snoring in her bed, and he was afraid it would cause too much trouble.

A loaf of dark bread lay in the center of the table. When had he seen bread like that, thick and crusty?

It was enough. That much would get them as far as the port and the ship.

He turned, and from the corner of his eye he saw a small tub of lard.

Lard smeared over bread.

Lard covering the tops of potatoes long ago, dripping over them.

Mam had made a sweet cake with lard once.

28

He took the tub, balanced it on top of the bread, and was reaching for the door when he heard heavy footsteps outside. Quickly he looked at the woman, but her head was buried under the coats. In two steps he was at the archway to the hall. He ran soundlessly, glancing up at the curved stairs, then darted through an open door into a room and almost without thinking crouched in back of a chair.

He heard someone knock at the kitchen door, and the woman grumbling. "Go away," she called.

The sound of his breath was loud in his ears. He leaned forward, his forehead against the back of the chair, gasping. But when no one came his breath slowed.

Windows lined one of the walls, and a path from the misty moon fell across the floor. He stood up and ran his fingers over the chair. It was covered in cloth that was soft against his rough fingers. On the other walls rows of books stretched to the ceiling. Hundreds of them.

Sean had never known anyone who owned a book. What was in those books? Francey had told him there were stories written down that could make you happy or sad just to know them. He said there were other things as well, things that would make you as smart as the English, and maybe as rich.

The thought came to him. Suppose he could read? It was such a strange thought that for a moment he forgot to be afraid. He pulled out a book and held it in his hand, feeling the leather cover that was as soft as the chair.

And then the cook stood there, framed in the doorway. "That was the gatekeeper," she said. "I've saved you once, but that is the end of it. You'll have to leave."

He placed the book in the space that was waiting for it and slid past her, the surge of fear back in his chest. He would have to pass the gatehouse to get to the road.

The moon had disappeared into the clouds and it had begun to rain, with large drops pelting the walkway. He pulled off his shirt to cover the bread and lard and started for the gates.

Lights flickered in the horse stalls, voices called, and there was the sound of a horse, its hooves grating on the gravel. Sean stepped back against one of the trees as the horse and rider thundered past. The gates swung open just long enough for them to go through before the guard closed them again.

He watched as the man went back to the gatehouse. He was shivering now; sheets of rain fell from the tree branches, soaking him. He waited, though. It was something else Francey had taught him: *Be patient, slow when you need to be.*

Soon the Englishman from the road would ride back through the gates. He'd remember Sean and let him out, waving his thanks. Sean huddled there thinking. It might not be like that. Suppose the man said, "I never told him he could have food"? The groomsman would be there, and the gatekeeper.

*Thief,* they'd say.

Francey had told him of people who had been sent on transports to a place called Australia for less than what he had taken, a place filled with convicts, a place so far away it was the opposite side of the earth. His mouth went dry, but he quieted himself with the thought that if he could get away from the Englishman's house, he and Mam and

Patch would eat enough to sleep through the night without hunger pains.

He left the shelter of the trees and skirted around the gatehouse to walk along the wall. Old vines clung to the slabs of stone, and he wondered if the thick branches would hold his weight. He made a bag of his shirt, knotting the sleeves together over the food, and walked a little farther.

He heard the horse returning but didn't stop to watch the guard come out of his house to open the gates. He reached for one of the branches and began to climb. Rolling himself over the top, he landed on his feet.

As he ran he heard voices and the sound of hooves. He veered off the path and saw the wee house where he had rested, a thin line of smoke coming from a hole in the roof. It was surprising to think they had fire, surprising too that they opened the door without even asking who was there. A man, bent and gray, stood there staring at him. In back of him a younger woman stood at the hearth.

Sean darted inside. "The Englishman," he said. "May I stay here for a few minutes?" He pointed to the bag he had made of his shirt. "I have bread. I'll give you a piece, both of you."

The man and woman looked at each other, and the man pointed to a loft so small it must have been used to hold the winter apples or oats in a better year.

He waited up there, careful not to crush the eggs, so cramped he couldn't stretch his legs. He worried about the time going, worried about the cart. No one came, not then nor later, and at last, in spite of himself, he slept.

He awoke with a start to peer over the edge of the loft, to see the man and woman asleep on the floor near-by.

He broke off a large chunk of the bread to leave for them, slid down the rope ladder, still careful of the eggs, and was out the door. It had not stopped raining, but it was a finer rain now, with fog all around him.

It was almost morning. He went back down the road, walking lightly on the balls of his feet. He felt rested, wide awake. He couldn't wait to show Mam and Patch the food he had for them.

It was a long distance, and after a while he wasn't sure if he had gone too far. Suppose they had dragged the cart off the road and were sleeping somewhere?

He decided to walk another bit, just for as long as it would take him to say the Our Father three times. But he was so worried he couldn't remember all of the prayer. "Give us this day our daily bread," he kept whispering to himself.

How could he have forgotten it, a prayer he had said all his life? And even after starting it over four or five times, he didn't see the cart, or Mam and Patch. At last he turned again to search the side of the road.

It was long after daybreak, and the fog had burned off. He sat down at the edge of the road wondering what to do. The great house was just over the rise, but by now he didn't think about anyone coming after him, or even care.

He couldn't remember crying, not once since he had been smaller than Patch. But now his throat burned and he could feel the same burning in his eyes. Where could they be?

Would he ever see Mam again? And hadn't he promised Nory he'd care for Patch?

He had a picture of Nory in his mind: Nory, younger with freckles dotting her nose. They were at Patrick's Well halfway up the cliff, and a red ribbon held back her hair. She had dared him to catch her, jumping from rock to rock, and he had reached out to pull at the ribbon. Caught by the wind, it had sailed toward the edge of the cliff. "Don't bother about it," she had said, but he had reached for it with outstretched fingers and tucked it in his pocket. He had it still after all this time.

How could he ever tell Nory that he had let something happen to Patch?

## SIX

### NORY

Who was watching her? She couldn't run from whoever it was, she knew that.

Anna's lined face came into her mind. Anna's angry face. *You have come this far. Be strong, child, fight back.*

Nory lay as still as she could, letting the person think she was asleep. At the same time she reached out around her, digging her fingers into the cold sand, searching for a rock or a shell. It would have to be something large enough to fell a man with one blow.

And there it was, a rock so large it would take both her hands to raise it. As he came nearer she'd roll over, her hands underneath it, and lift herself to her knees.

She'd have to do it in one sure motion, rolling, lifting, hurling it so hard he'd fall onto the sand, and somehow she'd crawl back to the road, back and back until there was somewhere to hide.

The man didn't move. He stayed there, bent almost double.

After a while her arms and legs ached from keeping them so rigid. Still he didn't come.

She watched him, trying not to blink for a long time, so long that at last her arms and legs went limp in spite of themselves. Her breath slowed, and there was a dream.

A ship was moving away from her. The path of water spread between the stern and the quay as it sailed toward the open sea. Someone held one hand out to her, calling, *Nory, Nory.*

And then she woke. The sky was a bowl of deepest blue, and a path of gold lay across the sea as the sun touched it. It seemed as if she might walk across it, dance across it.

She sat up awkwardly and ran her hands through the tangle of her hair, brushing out the sand. She thought she had never seen anything so beautiful as that sea and that day. But as she moved her foot she could feel the ache in it.

It all came back to her: her foot and then . . .

The man at the top of the hill!

She twisted around, but no one was there. Had she dreamed it?

And another thought. How could she walk the rest of the way? How far did she still have to go? She knew very little of this road, only that there was still most of Galway to be walked before she reached the ship.

She had to eat. She pulled the cloth bag up on her

lap and opened it, feeling two pieces of brack as hard as the stones on the road, and a bit of dried meat no larger than her thumb. *Oh, Anna, meat.*

She reached for a piece of brack, and as she took the first bite a shadow fell across the sand in front of her.

It was too late for the rock. Too late to scramble away.

Nory dropped the brack and stared up at a strange-looking girl, her face filthy, her curly hair thick and snarled, and so long it hid her eyes. Under her torn clothes with one sleeve almost gone, Nory could see the shape of her bones.

The girl scrambled over Nory's legs to reach for the brack. Without stopping to wipe off the sand, she bit into it, and before Nory could stop her, it was gone.

The girl licked her fingers, then ran her tongue over her lips, looking at the bag.

Quickly Nory pulled it under her skirt, then looked up. Suppose the girl found out about her foot! She glanced down at the piece of cloth that was wrapped around it, and with one hand she rearranged the fold of her skirt to cover it.

"You have something to eat," the girl said. "And I have had nothing this day." She grinned, showing darkened teeth. "Except for your miserable brack."

Nory narrowed her eyes. "I have nothing else for you," she said in her fiercest voice.

"I could take the bag," the girl said. "I don't think you can come after me."

"I won't let you."

"But I will not." The girl stood up, edging her foot toward Nory's skirt, lifting a bit of the hem with her toes. "You are trying to get to the port," she said. "But you might never get there with that."

She nudged Nory's foot with hers. "You with your wound that may fester." She leaned over. "You'll be lucky if it doesn't turn black."

"Black," Nory repeated, thinking of a woman in Ballilee who had somehow infected her leg on a wire fence. It *had* turned black, and grown to twice its size.

The girl pushed back her hair. "I'll reward you for your food. There's something I saw. . . ." She leaned forward, covering Nory's foot with the skirt again and giving it a small pat. She turned to wander along the edge of the water, following a piece of wood that was caught in the surf.

She called over her shoulder, "You were like a scrap of rag blown onto the sand, not worth a look. I watched you." She broke off as the plank was caught by an incoming wave, and reached out for it, soaking herself.

"There," she said, dragging the plank toward Nory. "You'll have something to lean on."

She stood there, still looking at the bag. "I should see if there's more food," she said. "But I won't." She showed those darkened teeth, almost smiling. Then she was gone, up and around the dunes toward the road.

# SEVEN

## SEAN

The day was full of wind: it tore up the sand in front of him and curled the waves back toward the sea. He found Mam's three-legged stool on the side of the road, hidden in the reeds and almost covered by the fine grains from the strand. Why was it there? What did it mean?

He might have stayed there forever, circling back and forth, knowing they had been there, asking people who shook their heads dumbly, but then he saw a girl who put out her hand. Her nails were cracked and broken and she looked as if she was starving.

The girl's face reminded him of his sister Mary's, the dark curly hair, the large eyes, but this girl's face was smooth, without the marks of the pox.

He broke off a small piece of the bread crust for her, lowering his head against the wind, feeling the grit in his eyes. "I have lost my family," he said, willing his mouth to stay firm, his eyes dry. "My mam and a small boy. They had a cart."

She closed her eyes, sucking on the bread. It took her a long time to swallow that wee bit, and she didn't answer until she had finished. "A cart," she said. "I think I saw a cart going south toward the port. A woman and a boy, maybe." She shrugged and held out her hand again. "Maybe it was a girl after all. I'm not sure."

Something was in his eye, scratching; he rubbed at it with his thumb, then broke off a second piece of bread, a piece no bigger than his thumbnail.

She put the bread in the sleeve of her dress, cupping her hands over her eyes, her long dark hair blowing against her face. "They were going down the road, each holding one of the cart poles. I don't know how long ago."

His eye was tearing now. He sank down on the ground, using the edge of his sleeve to get rid of the sand, then reached into his pocket to find something, anything, he could use to take it out.

"A ribbon!" she said. "Look."

He opened his eyes, squinting, to see Nory's ribbon caught by the wind, held against one of the reeds, then free again and blown across the strand.

He reached for it but then it was gone, with the girl scampering after it.

He stood there thinking about the ribbon and all he had lost. He could still feel the grain of sand in his eye. He picked up the three-legged stool and went on, walking the last miles, hurrying, sometimes running. He'd catch up with Mam and Patch. How much slower they'd be than he was, even though he kept crisscrossing the road, climbing the dunes, searching the water's edge. Why hadn't they waited for him? And he was tortured by worry: Maybe the cart the girl had seen hadn't been his cart at all.

Two days later he reached the port. His eye was still sore but the sand had washed itself out. He carried the stool over his head. He had thought about leaving it a dozen times. Once he had even set it down on the road, but he had gone back for it. When Mam had closed the door of the house for the last time she had taken it with her.

"There's no room on the cart," he had said. What was she thinking of?

She had shaken her head, her face rough. "It's what I have."

How unlike her it had seemed. Mam, who told him he was wasting time when he watched the sunlight sliding across the floor in patterns, who became angry when she saw him petting the goat's wiry head.

Her stool had rocked back and forth in the wagon. Pa had taken the wood from an old tree, cut it and smoothed it, and at the end carved a small rose in the center. Strange for him to remember Mam's words: *"It's what I have."*

How many of them had sat on that stool when they were all home, he or Francey, Liam, Michael, Mary, Da, or sometimes Granny, leaning a little to even it out on the rough earth of the floor. On dark evenings Granny had told stories, and so had Da, and he had listened, staring into the glow of the peat fire, seeing the shapes of the people they talked about there. A dreamer, they all called him, laughing.

All he had now. Even his ticket was gone, tucked in under a loose board in the cart.

He had eaten the Englishman's food, a little bit each time, saving some for when he found Mam and Patch. But the crumbs of bread and the lard that filled his stomach made him feel worse. Would he ever see them again?

On the pier below there was an explosion of noise and color. Men rolled barrels and shouted at each other. An endless line of people with packages and boxes, and even a few with squealing shoats in their arms, waited in front of an office door. Beyond them was the ocean, gray and angry as the rain began. The harbor was dotted with ships.

He went down the hill and wandered back and forth across the quay. Were Mam and Patch on one of those ships? And always he wondered: Why hadn't they waited for him?

He crouched on the filthy quay. Should he keep going? And how could he do that without a ticket?

He went to the line of people and stood at the end. The line moved slowly, and he began to talk with the man ahead of him. "It'll take two pounds for a ticket," the man said. "And they'll give you enough food and water to stay alive. Just alive."

Two pounds.

More money than he had seen in a lifetime.

He wandered off the line, the stool on his head protecting him from the driving rain. He tried to ignore a woman who called after him: "Thinks he's Queen Victoria, he does, with his own seat to perch on."

Ahead of him was a sailor, wearing a striped uniform

with bows fluttering from his cap. Sean followed him into a small shack and found a short line of men signing on for ship's work. All of them were older than he was; all of them acted as if they knew what they were doing.

"I'm a good worker," he said to the man in front of him, his mouth dry. "I need a job on a ship."

"So does every other man on this quay," the man said over his shoulder.

Sean waited anyway, until only that man was left in front of him. "There's a place for me on the *Clarence*," the man told the woman at the window. "O'Brian."

"Able-bodied seaman," she said, nodding. A paper was shoved out the window at the man, and he disappeared with it into the crowd.

And then it was Sean's turn. He looked up at the woman and was startled by what he saw. She was as large as any man, her face pitted with the marks of the pox much deeper than the small marks on Mary's cheeks. Her eyes were so small they almost disappeared into that massive flesh. "Well?" she asked, and even her voice was unusual, with an accent that wasn't familiar.

"I can do anything." He could hardly get out the words.

The woman, toothless, grinned at him. "Climb to the top of the mast in the midst of a storm?"

He nodded. "Anything."

"Next man," she said.

"Wait." He put the stool down and gripped the edge of her counter, feeling so dizzy he thought he might faint. "Please."

She looked down at the papers in front of her, shuffling them with dirty fingers. "Why should I give you something?"

He shook his head, trying to think of a reason. "Food," he said, knowing he wasn't making sense; he had none of the Englishman's food left, and hadn't eaten today. Then he saw her looking at the stool in front of him, Ma's stool with the small rose in the center.

She pointed at it with one massive finger.

He knew what she wanted. She would give him passage in return for the stool. He had no choice. *Ah, Mam*, he thought. Then he nodded at the woman.

She raised her eyebrows, shuffled the papers one more time. "Cook? Is that it?"

"No, I . . . ," he began, remembering Mam draining the potatoes in the rush basket. He didn't know one thing about cooking food. "Yes. I will cook."

She looked up at him from under bushy eyebrows. "The pay," she said, "is just a few coins for the whole trip."

"Yes."

"Cook's assistant," she said.

"Yes."

She jerked her head. "Bring the stool around the back." But as she pushed a paper through the bars at him she said, "There's something first, though."

Sean leaned forward.

"Ballast," she said. "You'll have to act as ballast on the *Manchester* to Liverpool. The ship will be in soon." Her eyes slid away from him. "The cargo of the *Manchester* is no longer . . ." She hesitated. "Alive."

Sean's eyes widened.

"Pigs," she said. "Diseased. They were cast into the ocean."

"What's ballast?" he began, but already she was waving him away.

He picked up the papers and backed away from her.

"Ballast?" he heard someone say. "I wouldn't do that if I had to lie down dead in the street instead."

Sean shrugged. What difference did it make?

## EIGHT

### NORY

Nory watched the road beneath her; it was swept with sand in patches, or mud where the sea had reached it at high tide. Once she stopped to pick up a blue stone, the color of Patch's eyes.

*Oh, Patch,* she thought, remembering.

"I will give you my best blue stone, Nory, because you are my best sister."

"I thought it was Maggie."

He had shaken his head, his hair swirling.

"Well, Celia then."

"Never."

Patch with the blue stone eyes.

She stopped to rest often, but she was careful to choose a spot out of the way, where no one would see her. Once she traced the letters on the plank the girl had given her. English letters, English words. Granda knew all of them. He had fought in a war long ago and had traveled all over speaking that language. She knew some letters, of course. The *R*, the letter that began her last name, *Ryan*, and an *S* too. She had seen Sean Red scratch his own name in the earth often enough. What had he said?

"When I'm rich someday, Nory, I'll buy a writing stick, and silk paper."

"How are you going to be rich, Sean Red?"

"I will get me a farm in Brooklyn, America, and have fields of food to sell." He had waggled his eyebrows at her. "If you are lucky, I might give you a head of cabbage or a bit of garlic to hang around your neck."

"*Fuafar* garlic! Keep it for your own self."

She traced a third letter with her finger. It was a pointy roof without a house to go with it, and she thought it might be in her own Ryan name but she couldn't remember.

She sat back, wondering about the plank and its letters. Could it be from a ship? Why was it floating along by itself in the surf? What might have happened to that ship and all the people who were on it?

She thought instead of the girl with the blackened teeth and the curly hair who had taken her food and left her the plank.

With the plank she was able to hobble along. The rough wood bruised the soft skin under her arm and blistered her fingers, but by the second day she could feel the pull in her foot as the cut slowly began to heal. All she had to do, she told herself, was to climb one more hill, to circle around one more curve in the road.

Sometimes as she walked she lifted her head to watch the birds wheeling far up over the sea. She always hoped to see the white bird and remind it of the biscuit, but all she saw were the smaller, darker cliff birds. She tried not to think of the food the bird had dropped into the sea. Did it mean bad fortune for her journey? Bad fortune for Sean Red, for Patch, for Granda, Celia, and Da?

She moved around a mother and a little girl huddled together. The daughter mumbled something and was still again.

Nory knew she had to sleep; it was hard to keep her eyes open. But the place she chose had to be away from those who might take her bag or her shawl while she slept. She looked for somewhere in the dunes where she could hide, or for boreens, those small paths that led away from the sea. She even followed one for a short distance, but nowhere seemed safe.

At first there were still people to be seen. A couple crouched in the high grass and stared at her as she passed. And down below women searched uselessly for food at the water's edge.

By the time she reached the top of the boreen and the ruined shed she was alone. Here the sound of the sea was muted; there was only the swish of the sea grass as it rubbed against the stones of the shed. The field was picked bare, no plants showing their leaves, no lazy beds of potatoes, only a cart with one of its wheels propped up against it.

She slipped into the shed, ducked under the pieces of roof that had fallen inside, and rolled herself tight in one corner with the bag in back of her. It would be hard for anyone to see her, she told herself.

She fell asleep looking up at the sky with its dark gray clouds and the threat of rain and dreamed of Granda telling her the story of white birds, and strange worlds under the sea.

# NINE

## SEAN

It was dark in the hold of the ship, but not the same darkness Sean remembered on moonless nights in Maidin Bay. At home, as he stood in front of the house, his eyes would become used to the lack of light. He'd see the outline of the cliffs against the sky first, and then the stone walls of Nory's house, and the shape of the boreen that led to Anna's.

But this!

It was as if he were blind. If he raised his hand in front of his eyes, he wouldn't be able to see his fingers or the shadow of his sleeve.

But he couldn't even raise his arms. Men stood on each side of him so packed in, he could hardly move. The water sloshed back and forth against his legs.

How long had he stood like this, unable to sink down to rest? Hours? Days? Forever?

How had he gotten himself to this? Lost Mam, lost little Patch, lost the cart?

Around him was noise: the sound of men coughing, moaning, and from somewhere in back of him, someone was crying, a deep sobbing coming from his chest, and that sound went on and on. "This ship used to carry slaves," someone said. "And now it carries the Irish."

It was almost as if he himself were crying. He took the same deep breaths the man took, could feel the same crying inside.

Next to him a man was talking. Talking to him?

"My name is Garvey, cook's assistant. And I will get through this somehow."

"I am Mallon," Sean said. "They call me Sean Red."

"But they call us ballast," the man said. "Taking the place of whatever the ship was carrying on the way over. Taking the weight of it. We're not men. We're sheep or cattle or crates of wine to the English. We're what keeps the ship from turning on her side."

Sean had known only two Englishmen: Lord Cunningham in Ballilee, and the one with the boots on the road. Once he and Nory had seen the inside of Cunningham's house. It was because of a dare.

"Climb the great wall," she had said. "You'll never do it."

So he'd done it, of course, and from the top of the wall he had dared her to creep up through the avenue of great trees. Together, breathless, they had come out at the very front of the house and ducked down in the shelter of the vines to look in the glass windows.

The room inside was larger than his own house. The table in the center was the color of Anna's blackthorn cane but gleamed in the light, shiny and smooth, and the chair legs were carved into the shapes of claws.

"Wake up, lad," Garvey said next to him. "You're leaning on me."

"Sorry," he said, trying to straighten himself. He remembered he had touched those windows, run his fingers over them, almost as if he were running his hands over that great table.

He thought then of the Englishman with the boots, and his room filled with books that stretched as high as the ceiling.

"What would someone do with all those books?" Nory would have asked.

The walls of his own house were made of thick stones that had come out of the fields so long ago no one could remember when. Pa had whitewashed them with lime every year on St. Bridget's Eve. By the next year, most of the lime was gone, and the stones had a greenish look to them. There were nails dug into the grout around the stones. And hung on those nails . . .

"Wake up," Garvey said again.

. . . were fishing lines and a pail, the rush basket for potatoes. The loy for digging. Francey's boots with holes in the soles. An old cap.

They were all still there, would stay there until someone came to tumble the house.

"What did you say?" Garvey asked.

Sean shook his head. In his head he began to count the books on the wall of the Englishman's house. Suppose there were fifty on each shelf? Suppose there were ten shelves, twenty shelves?

He couldn't count that. He could do ten and ten, his

fingers, his toes, twenty, the number of rocks that made up the low stone wall in front of his house.

He was falling asleep again. And then the thought came to him as it had in the Englishman's house. Suppose he could read what was in those books?

"What?" Garvey asked.

"Read," Sean said, his tongue thick.

"Ah, now," Garvey said. "There are few that can do that."

"I know my name," Sean said. "There's an *S*, and an *E*." He was too tired to remember the rest.

He didn't have to. Suddenly there was a grinding sound, as if the ship had struck something. The hatch cover was opened, and light streamed down on top of him.

Blinding light.

He closed his eyes against it.

"We're here," Garvey said. "We did it."

Sean opened his eyes, blinking, and waited his turn to climb, wondering if his legs would hold him.

Still he thought about the letters of his name and all the books in the Englishman's house. He thought of Brooklyn and his family waiting for him: gentle Mary, Francey, Nory's Maggie. And where were Mam and little Patch?

If only they were safe somewhere.

He promised himself he'd find them someday.

He thought of books then. Someday he'd have a book for himself, too, and he'd be able to read it, one page after another.

## TEN

Her mouth was dry. "Celia," she called to her sister. "Just a cup of hot water from the hearth."

"Am I your servant then?" Celia asked.

"I'll sing you a song for a swallow of water."

"Do you think I have time for singing now?" But Celia held out the cup.

As Nory reached for it a drop splashed onto her chin, and another onto her nose. "How can I sing if I'm drowning?" she asked.

Celia was laughing. Nory could hear the sound of it, like the patter of soft rain at Patrick's Well. She raised her hand to wipe her face, then opened her eyes.

There was more water on her face now, and she wondered if she was crying. It was dark, and she turned her head to look at the banked fire in the hearth. After a moment she realized where she was.

Not home with Celia.

No hearth to spread its warmth.

No Patch in the middle of their straw bed.

She was alone, and the drops she felt on her face were drops of rain coming down into the shed without its roof. She opened her mouth to catch some of the water. It washed her cracked lips and ran down her throat, and she kept swallowing, feeling the thirst leaving her.

She pulled some of the thatch around her, thinking about the food that was left: a mouthful of brack and that wee bit of dried meat. Should she eat now? There was a tapping somewhere in back of her eyes, so it was hard to think.

She heard something, not the rain. She lay very still, listening. Was it the sound of geese honking?

She sat up carefully. It almost sounded like the rough voice of a woman. A woman crying?

Just the wind. Only the wind.

She reached into the bag and took out the brack. She felt the hard crust in her fingers, the center slightly softer. She remembered Anna at the hearth swinging the pot over the fire, making brack. Before that it was her sister Maggie stirring the flour and water: *"Just so, Nory. Don't work it too much, only enough to make a smooth round loaf."*

Maggie in America.

Nory took the tiniest bite of brack, saving the rest of it. She felt the bit of meat in the bag, and then the small bags of leaves and seeds Anna had given her. Leaves and seeds for cures.

The thatch was damp and her clothes were cold and

wet. It must be almost morning. She'd start now in the early darkness and get that much closer to the port.

She reached for the plank and left the shed. The rain was ending, and a faint hint of light came across the edge of the field to the east.

There it was, that crying again.

It came from the cart in the center of the field. Hearing Anna's voice in her mind, *Keep going, keep going,* she turned her back and started for the boreen.

The woman was crying, she told herself, because the wheel of the cart had come off. There was nothing she could do to help.

Celia would have helped. Maggie would have helped. Granda . . .

She turned as the woman came around the side of the cart. A big woman, rough-looking.

She drew in her breath.

It was Sean Mallon's mam. Sean's cart then?

And another breath.

Patch must be nearby.

She hobbled toward the cart, the plank digging into her arm, but she had no time to think about that. She went faster, stumbling; it was hard to breathe.

"Nora?" the woman was saying. "Nora?"

She found him lying on the edge of the cart, his legs drawn up, his arms covering his head. Small puddles of rain had gathered in his clothes.

She dropped the stick and pulled herself up on the cart to kneel awkwardly beside him, reaching out to touch that bony back, the bitten nails, the freckles on the side of his face.

He never woke but he moved closer to her. She

gathered him up, feeling how cold he was, and sat there rocking back and forth, holding him against the dampness and the wind that was sweeping across the field.

And the woman's voice again. "Nora. How can it be?"

Patch stirred in Nory's arms. "We'll see 416 Smith Street," she whispered. "And we'll knock on the door, all of us holding hands. And when Maggie opens it . . ."

She spoke calmly, but her heart was beating so fast in her throat she could hardly swallow. She had to get him warm.

She looked up at Mrs. Mallon. Here was someone to take care of Patch, to take care of her. Not to be alone. How strange. Wanting Mrs. Mallon to take care of them, Mrs. Mallon who was rough and often un-friendly. Nory remembered her chasing the pig in the field, yelling at her sons, never laughing. But now for the first time she thought of her as a mother. Sean's mother.

Nory looked around, rubbing Patch's arms, his legs. "Where is Sean then? What has happened?"

Mrs. Mallon shook her head. Once she had been stout with plump cheeks, but now her skin sagged and was the color of old milk.

"Where is Sean?" Nory asked again.

Mrs. Mallon shook her head slowly. "He was to go for food, but he never came back that night. I tried to pull the cart away, tried to hide it. I dragged it all the way up here, but you can see what has happened to it." She looked over her shoulder at it. "I have been down at the edge of the sea all night trying to find something for us to eat." She stopped to run her hand over her face, and when she spoke again Nory could hardly hear her. "Sean is dead," she said. "He must be dead."

Nory could feel the strength go out of her own legs, out of her hands and her fingers. "How long ago?"

"Days. And I will not go to America without him."

Mrs. Mallon's eyes were so sad Nory could hardly look at her.

Sean, who had danced with her at Maggie's wedding. Sean, who had promised to take care of Patch. Sean, who would be there if he could. Sean, who someday might have been her husband. She tried to swallow.

"What will we do?" Nory asked.

"I don't know." Mrs. Mallon shook her head slowly.

"Please . . . ," Nory began, then took a breath. In her arms Patch was the size of a child half his age. She reached into the bag for the piece of brack and held it up to him. "Open your mouth," she said.

She fed it to him, a few crumbs small enough for the sparrows that nested in the hedges at home, and he never once opened his eyes. She saw Mrs. Mallon bite her lip and look away.

Anna had given Patch milk once, and stared her down, knowing she wanted milk too. "You are strong," Anna had said, and given all of it to him.

"I have no food to spare," Nory told Mrs. Mallon. "What I have is not for you or me. It is for him." She thought about the meat, but she'd wait to give it to him later in the morning, or even when the sun went down, to hold him through the night.

Mrs. Mallon sat opposite them, her hands pulling at a clump of grass.

"I will help you fix the cart somehow," Nory told her. "And we'll go on."

"Go on?" Mrs. Mallon put a blade of grass into her mouth. "I tried to pull the cart over a rock and now the axle is broken. It will be here until someone cuts into it for firewood and the nails rust away in the field."

Nory took a breath. "I'll carry Patch then."

Mrs. Mallon looked at the board and then at her foot. "You will never—"

"I will," Nory said, hearing Anna's voice in her head. "My foot is better now. I won't need the board."

"I will walk back to my house in Maidin Bay," Mrs. Mallon said. "I won't be alone. Anna is there still. If I don't die on the road, I will die at my hearth."

Nory shook her head. "The roof will be tumbled. Your house will be finished, and the English will never let you stay there. Come with me. Together—"

But Mrs. Mallon went to the cart and came back with pieces of paper fluttering in her hands. "Papers that would have taken us on a ship to America," she said. "I won't need them. Sean won't. But Patch . . ." She handed them to Nory, then touched the top of her head as she went heavily past her down the boreen and was gone.

"Don't go," Nory called after her. "Please stay with us. Please . . ."

She shivered. Could Mrs. Mallon really be gone? Had she really left them? Nory closed her eyes, thinking of Anna and then Granda.

"Patch, you are a great boy, *a stór,*" Nory said, turning back to him. "You will put your arms around my neck and your head on my shoulder. You will hold on to me and I will take you to the ship, and to Maggie."

## ELEVEN

### SEAN

Liverpool. A strange word, an English word. Streets were filled with lodging for those who had money. Men in aprons sold skillets, and pots, and blankets so thin Sean could see through them. Great crowds of people wandered among carts and bales of hay. Men shouted, animals lowed, and in the harbor were great ships. People around them were speaking in English, that strange language.

He breathed in the smells of the water, and filth, and food. Food was being sold from carts and small tents.

If only he could have a bite of bread, a potato, or a bit of fish.

Garvey stood next to him.

Sean took a breath. "I must find my family," he said. "They're ahead of me somewhere, I think." His mother was strong. He held on to that. He looked away so Garvey couldn't see his eyes.

Garvey scratched one of his large ears. "You'd have to look at every face, every soul who is here in Liverpool, and it seems as if it is the entire world." He put his hand on Sean's shoulder. "I will spend my last wee bit of money on a fish that swam in the sea this morning and jumped into the net with me on his mind."

His brothers had caught fish in their curragh, Sean thought, white-bellied fish that they salted and mixed with potatoes. But that was before the potatoes had failed. That was before the English had taken their sturdy curragh and locked it on the quay to pay the rent.

Garvey turned aside to dicker with a woman over the price of the fish. He came back a moment later, pulling the fish apart in his hands, and gave a strip to Sean.

Sean took it in his hands, feeling the softness of it, smelling the sea in it. He held it in his mouth then, not chewing. He had never tasted anything as good as that bit of fish on his tongue, against his teeth, on the roof of his mouth. "I thank you, Garvey," he said.

But Garvey was pointing. "The ship!"

An old dark ship, Sean thought, with sails limp and clinging to the wooden masts, as if they had no strength left in them. And the name? He spelled out the letters: *S*, the start of his own name, *A*, a pointed letter, an *M*, *S* for *Sean* again, a circle for *O*, ending with an *N* for *Nory*.

A good omen, their names together on the back of the ship. It was almost as if the letters would push him across the sea.

"The *Samson*," Garvey said. "It will take us to America."

## TWELVE

### NORY

She wondered at herself that she could do this, leave the plank on the side of the road, put the weight of her foot on those hard stones, carry Patch, her bag slung over her shoulder, and keep going hour after hour. A day. Two days. But she did do it, and she knew she would reach the port.

She thought of Mrs. Mallon taking that long walk back to Maidin Bay. Did she have the strength for it?

It was almost dark now, and she sang for Patch as she walked, the sound in her throat dry at first, but gathering strength: *"Wee melodie man, the rumpty tumpty toddy man."*

She wanted to cry for Sean, but something had happened to her eyes. They were dry and burning, and the tears that would have bathed them wouldn't come. And always there were pictures in her mind of Mrs. Mallon handing her the papers for the ship, papers that were like the ones Da had sent her.

Sometimes Patch spoke a few words in a rusty little voice, and she tried to question him. "You saw an Englishman?"

"Yes, with boots," he said. "And I too . . ." His voice trailed off.

She finished it for him. "Yes, someday in America you will have boots."

What had Sean said? *I will have fields and I will give you cabbage and a clove of garlic.*

"And what did the Englishman tell you?" she asked.

"He would give us food," Patch said. "I think colcannon."

Nory closed her eyes, remembering her sister Maggie as she stirred milk and butter into soft white potatoes and cabbage.

"Tell the rest of it," she said as she tried to shift his weight.

Patch grasped her shoulders with both hands. "No rest of it. No colcannon, and the cart turned over."

He was quiet then. His head went down against her back and she knew he was asleep. She went on, head bent, watching for rocks and stones in the road, telling herself she could take one step and another, just one more, just two more, climb the next hill, inch her way down the other side. Her shoulders ached from the weight of Patch, but the cut on her foot was healing, and in spite of everything she felt happy, glad that Patch was with her, glad that she had found him. But how sorry she was that Mrs. Mallon hadn't come with them.

Once she sank down at the side of the road and fed

him the rest of the meat. The next day she pulled the stitches from her cape until the small coin that Anna had given her dropped into her fingers. From an old woman she exchanged it for a stale piece of brack, which she and Patch shared.

On the third day he was awake again, pointing. "Look, Nory."

"Galway," she breathed.

Below them houses leaned together on the streets. More houses than she had ever seen before! Flickering flames from candles glowed in windows so that everything shimmered. And the tart smell of peat fires was everywhere.

She stood there, Patch in her arms, wondering at the size of it all. Then she walked on until the road curved and the port was spread out in front of them. Da had told her about that port and the fishing ships he had sailed, wresting the great cod out of the water to bring in the rent money. But Da had made her imagine it in the light of day with the sun dancing on the water and white sails shimmering like the wings of that great seabird.

Instead she stumbled onto the pier with Patch in the middle of the night to see water, ghostly in the fog, the hulks of ships anchored outside the harbor, and strange shapes everywhere like the *bean sídhe* who warned of death.

But somewhere there, right in front of them perhaps, was her family: Celia with her turned-up nose, Granda with his white beard and his head full of stories for her, Da with his smiling eyes.

The day before he had left for the fishing trip she

had walked with Da. A bone cold day it had been, and she had slipped her hand in his, feeling the size of it, the warmth. He had promised her it would be only months until he'd be home with pockets jingling.

He had never been able to come, though, not in more than a year, but he was waiting for her here.

Bundles were piled in doorways and out in the open. Nory stumbled against one of them and realized the bundles were alive. People were sleeping there, whole families.

"Da," she said as loud as she could, and Patch said it too, his soft breath against her neck. She called until her voice was hoarse, and the bundles around them stirred angrily, but no one answered her. People began to mutter and she knew it was the sound of her voice that kept them awake. Someone threw a stone that glanced off the side of her bag and hit a wall in back of them.

At last they sank down in a rough spot at the corner of a building. Nory pulled her bag in between the two of them, and she held Patch's hand across the top of it to keep it safe. Patch was asleep almost at once, his pale eyelashes down over his cheek.

She watched him, remembering when he was just beginning to walk, his cheeks round, his legs sturdy, as she held him up. But now his cheeks were sunken, his freckles standing out in that white face, and his legs were nothing but bones.

*Tomorrow*, she told herself. *Somehow* . . . Her eyes fluttered closed and she slept until just before dawn, when the harbor came to life.

Bundles moved, changed shapes, people called out to each other. "A ship," someone cried.

Nory turned. Their ship?

It had been on Nory's mind all the time she had walked from Maidin Bay. Shining, clean and white, sails billowing. A sight that would never be forgotten.

But this? Anchored just outside the harbor, dirty gray, pails of bilge water cascading over the side. That couldn't be her ship, could it?

She leaned over as a man went by. "Where is that ship going?"

He looked after it. "Where most of them go. First to Liverpool, and then to America or Canada." He shrugged. "Or down to the bottom of the sea."

"Will there be food?" she asked.

"Not yet," the man said. "The ship will take you to Liverpool first, and you must have your own food until you board the ship there that will take you to the Americas."

Nory's stomach lurched from hunger. Next to her Patch had awakened too. His lips were dry and his head was back against the building. He had to have something to eat. It would have been better, she thought, if he had pulled at her skirt and cried for food, but he was too weak even for that.

A long, ragged line was forming at the edge of the quay. Small boats kept filling with people; then sailors rowed them out to the ship.

Where was Da? she wondered. Where were Granda and Celia?

At the head of the line an old woman screamed as a

sailor tried to push her onto one of the boats. Nory could see she was terrified of the rough water that splashed up between the quay and the small boat. And to get onto the boat she'd have to jump that distance.

The woman grasped a wooden post with one hand. "I can't," she wailed.

"How do you think you're going to get out to the ship, old shawlie?" the sailor asked, laughing. "It's not going to scrape the bottom of the harbor to come in for you."

Still the old woman hesitated.

"You're holding us up." He grabbed her arms and in one motion tossed her into the boat.

Nory's hand went to her face as the woman landed painfully in the bottom and lay there sobbing, her long skirt soaked with the filthy water that sloshed back and forth between the seats.

"This is just the beginning." The sailor shrugged. "What do you think it's like on the ocean with waves thirty feet high?" He called across to another sailor, "It will take hours to get these people out there. Like frightened rabbits they are, not one backbone in a hundred."

Patch pulled on her hand. "On our ship, Nory," he asked, "will we have food?"

Was that their ship? She felt for the pieces of paper in her bag and held them out to the sailor.

He shook his head, barely looking at them.

She leaned against a cold stone building, almost in a daze for want of food and trying to decide what to do.

Rough men wheeled heavy barrels around her. Women begged for food, hands out. Another ship, smaller than the first, had come into the harbor, and knots of people had somehow become another uneven line waiting to board. She held out the papers to another sailor, only to have him brush past her. "No," he said.

She watched all of what was going on for a long time, eyes half closed, until someone threw a pail of water out the window over her head. She jumped when it splattered in front of her, and Patch began to cry, a small whimpering cry without tears.

*Women begging for food.*

They had been hungry, all of them in the little house outside of Ballilee. One after another they had left that house until at last Nory had been alone with Anna. She had scaled the cliffs for eggs. She had gathered wee bits of grass and leaves and stirred them into something that couldn't even be called soup, but never once had she thought of begging.

*Begging.*

"Don't move," she told Patch. "Sit right here in this space. I'll be back soon."

She moved closer to the line of people boarding the small boats and stood to the side, one hand out, looking at each face as the line meandered past her. "Please," she said, hearing the shame of it in her voice. "Help me."

Someone pushed a shawl into her hand. It was a colorless wrap, thinner, older, dirtier than the one she wore. "Take it, poor creature," the woman said.

Nory thought of what her sister Celia would say: *Don't touch that, it's filthy.* Fuafar!

She took a breath. "Food?" she asked the woman. "Do you have just a bit for my wee brother? He doesn't need much."

The woman shook her head, gathering two of her own children around her, and moved away.

One woman put a small cracked cup into her hand. "We won't need this," she said. "We're going to start over."

Nory looked down at the cup. She would take it with her. Poor cup that no one wanted. She'd set it on Maggie's table at 416 Smith Street in Brooklyn and tell her sister all that had happened.

Nory felt hands on her shoulders. Slowly she raised her own hands to touch those hands, and knew without even lifting her head who it was.

Had she not seen those hands all her life? Hands baiting the hooks to catch a fish for their dinner. Hands digging the potatoes in the field, turning over the earth. Evenings of storytelling as he tamped weeds into his old pipe.

The woman's shawl slid out of her hand, and she caught the cup just in time. She turned and her arms went around the tall man with the untrimmed beard. But how thin he was, rail thin, his frame nothing but bones under her hands.

"Granda," she said, her face buried in his frieze jacket.

They stood there holding each other, Nory crying as Granda whispered to her, "I have searched every face for you and for Patch. I knew I would find you." He patted her shoulder. "I have not slept, so anxious I was to find you in the midst of all these travelers."

She took a breath. "Da," she said, "and Celia. Where are they? I can't wait to see them."

He shook his head. "I must tell you about them."

She nodded slowly. Something was wrong. She reached down for the shawl that lay against her feet. "I will take you to Patch," she said.

THE SHIP

## THIRTEEN

### NORY

After they found Patch, Granda took the filthy shawl she had gotten from begging and dropped it into the water. It bobbed along, a bubble on the foam. "Fleas," he said. "Tiny insects that crawl out of seams and devil and bite." He patted Nory's face. "The cup with its wee roses we'll keep for a sip of tea at Maggie's."

"But what about Da and Celia?" she asked at last.

She felt the tears in her eyes as Granda traced the same route she and Patch had taken with his broad fingers against her bag. "It was here," he said, "that your sister Celia and I rested, here that a man gave us a piece of fish, just gave it to us and went on, and here that Celia cried for you and wanted to turn back."

He patted Patch's head. "We found your da at last on the road overlooking the port."

Nory closed her eyes as she heard the story of Celia and Da twirling together, laughing, sobbing, dancing.

"Where are they?" Nory said.

Granda leaned forward. "Ah, they have gone ahead days ago."

Nory sat back. She couldn't believe it. Gone to America? Gone without them?

"But why?" She kept shaking her head, waiting for Granda to say he was only teasing.

"Days were written on those bits of paper," Granda began.

"The tickets," she said.

"And those days had come, the ticket seller told us. Two had to go. One could stay." He held out his broad hands. "Each of us wanted to be the one to wait for you, your da saying he had thought of seeing you every day for a year, Celia saying it was her right as your sister."

He smiled at her. "But we all knew your da shouldn't delay. He had to get to America, find work to take care of us all." He reached out to touch her shoulder. "I would be the one who waited. Who could love you and Patch more? I told them I would find you and take care of you with all the strength I had."

He took Nory's hand in one of his and Patch's hand in the other, his face grim. "And now we'll go to the ticket office."

The building was a poor shack, Nory thought. It looked as if it had been slapped up in a moment. Inside there were so many people in line or leaning against the walls that she wondered if the whole thing might collapse.

But Granda somehow got them through and up to the very front, where a man sat in back of an iron cage.

At first he didn't look up. He fingered the piles of tickets, stacks of papers, and rows of shiny coins piled up on one another. Then at last he told them to slide their own tickets through a space in the bars. Nory glanced up at Granda. Suppose this man took their tickets and never gave them back?

But they did as he told them. The man took the tickets, turning them one way and then another.

"There are extra papers there," Nory said. "Not used. They were for my friends. Can I give them to someone?"

"Useless," the man said. "All of them. The time has passed for these." Before Nory's eyes, he slipped all of the tickets into a drawer. He turned to Granda. "Do you have money?"

Granda closed his eyes as Nory looked up at him, holding her breath. Suppose they were in this place forever?

She could feel herself trembling. She clenched her hands tightly together. Suppose they were left here on this quay, too far to go home again, left to starve.

But Granda reached into his pocket. "I have a few coins," he said, and slid them under the bars.

"We have come so far," Nory said at the same time, "all the way from Ballilee, on our way to Brooklyn, New York. And the rest of our family has already left."

The man looked at the coins again. He paused, then finally said, "There's a ship leaving from Liverpool called the *Samson.*"

"Where do we go?" Granda asked. "Which line?"

"Yes, the *Samson*," the man said. "A couple from the Glenties, near Ballilee, just came through." He pointed. "The woman has a hat with roses. You see? Going across the quay. You can follow them right along." He swept Granda's coins into his tray and pulled three papers in front of him.

Nory was filled with such relief she felt her legs grow weak. She held on to the bars to keep herself up.

Just then as the man bent over to scribble on one of his papers, someone leaned over Nory's shoulder; a thin hand reached through the ticket seller's bars and with one finger scooped out two coins.

Had Nory seen that? Had she really seen someone steal money right under the ticket seller's eyes? Next to her Patch gave her hand a quick tug. He had seen the same thing!

She turned to look over her shoulder straight into the dark eyes of a girl.

That girl.

The one who had stolen her food and left the plank.

The girl raised her eyebrows, staring back at her, but the man pushed three tickets out at Granda. "Find the line for a trip to Liverpool," he said.

"But we're going to Brooklyn," Nory said.

Granda took her arm to lead her away. "Liverpool is on the way." He bent over to whisper to her. "Strange people, these English. Their ships go all the way back to England before we sail to America."

"I have money," the girl was saying in her harsh voice. "I want to pay for a ticket."

"Where are you going?" the ticket seller asked.

"To my brother Owen," she said. "I think he's in a place called New Jersey."

Nory covered her mouth with one hand. The girl was buying a ticket with the ticket seller's own money. But Nory didn't have time to think about it. Granda was rushing them along the quay, following the woman in the hat with the roses.

Up close Nory could see the hat was ancient. It was drenched with rain, the roses faded and drooping. The woman and her husband were surrounded by bags and old boxes.

"Casey is our name," the woman said.

It was the Caseys who got them through that terrible trip from Galway to Liverpool on the deck of a rusty, listing boat that must have been years older than Granda. They found a spot out of the wind and huddled together. Mrs. Casey comforted them. "In America it will all be different. We will sleep on a silk mattress with the softest pillows made of goose feathers." She laughed. "Do we know that America has geese? They might have other fowl, even softer."

All the while she was holding a bag. "Put your hand in this bag, my girl," she told Nory.

"Not I." The bag moved and jumped as if it had a life of its own.

The Caseys laughed, and Patch leaned forward, watching as Mrs. Casey took Nory's hand and guided it carefully into the cloth bag.

It *did* have a life of its own! Inside was a soft snuffling snout and small pointy ears. Nory felt the papery tongue and the mouth that nibbled on her fingers.

She pulled out her hand. "What is that?"

"One wee piglet," Mrs. Casey said. "I scooped her up from the landlord's sty."

"Stole?" Nory asked.

"Ah, no. It was a runty pig and the landlord gave her to me. He thought the pig wouldn't last a day."

Mrs. Casey threw back her head, her gray hair swinging. "He was wrong. I fed the pig better than I fed the landlord himself."

Nory put her hand back into the bag to scratch the pig's wiry little neck, then gave Patch a turn. "We had a pig," she said. "A great pig." She sighed, thinking about the *swish-swish* sound as Muc rubbed her sides against her pen. Poor Muc, gone to the English to pay the rent.

"I earned this pig," Mrs. Casey said. "I worked in the man's kitchen from before light in the morning until it was so dark I couldn't see the table in front of me, scrubbing, cutting, chopping, boiling, baking. But no more."

Mrs. Casey leaned closer, her pale blue eyes gleaming. "The pig and I walked out. Now the landlord will have to cut and chop and boil his own meals if he wants to eat."

Through the rain that spat at them on the rusty deck, the Caseys told stories about the landlord and the Glenties. And even after they arrived in Liverpool and waited to board the *Samson*, they talked of the fairs they had been to before the potatoes had failed, and how Mrs. Casey had found her hat on a fence post years ago.

And then at last they were wedged in their berths on the *Samson*, the ship that would take them to America:

Granda on top with the Caseys, Nory below with Patch and a girl named Lally who was going to be a maid in a great house in New York.

That first night Nory drifted off to sleep thinking nothing could happen with Granda there. And hadn't she always loved the sea? The ship would glide through it and at last she'd be in Brooklyn with everyone she loved. *Celia and Da twirling in the road.* How lovely to think of it.

She wasn't even that hungry. When they had boarded the *Samson* they'd been given food. A thin-faced boy with jug ears named Garvey had handed them bags of meal and biscuits.

No matter that they'd waited in line for hours to cook the oatmeal on the passengers' stove on the fore-deck. No matter that all of it had been gone in moments and they had licked their fingers, wishing for another mouthful.

One tiny bit of the meal was left on the side of Patch's cheek. Nory had reached out with her finger to slide it into his mouth, then patted that cheek.

"Is this the only food we will have for the whole voyage, your honor?" Nory asked the boy with the huge ears.

Garvey plucked at his red shirt, looking important, but then he laughed. "I'm not your honor," he said. "I'm just a steward—not even that, cook's assistant. And there will be a little food in the morning. Every morning." He'd leaned forward. "But the meal will be full of bugs."

*What are a few wee mealy bugs?* she thought.

"There will be stoves on the deck, not many, but you

may be able to cook your meal." He smiled, pulling at one ear. "And the wee bugs as well."

And then they were moving, with a terrible grinding. By morning there were other sounds that never stopped: so many people, women sighing, crying out in their sleep, babies wailing, one of them day and night, and poor Granda coughing. But the worst was the vomiting that went on and on.

And once, just for the barest beat, the *Samson* seemed to pause in the waves, to lurch like a man with a cane. Patch, next to her, held her arm with a strength Nory couldn't believe was his. "Are we sinking?" he asked, his teeth clenched.

Nory was so terrified she couldn't answer.

"We are just out of the harbor," Granda said. "It's all right."

The next day Nory felt a lurch in her own stomach. The light was dim in the moving, rocking cabin; nothing was still. Everything had a terrible smell of old food, or old clothes, and someone must have been sick. Seasick, she told herself.

She wouldn't think about the slosh of water against the side of the ship, the smells, the swaying from side to side. She'd lie still so she wouldn't wake Patch next to her; she'd try to stop rocking with the ship. Her forehead was filmy with sweat and her hands were damp. She was going to be sick too. But there was no place to be alone.

She sat up, her head hitting the top of the bunk, and slid onto the floor. In one terrible moment she lost the food that Garvey had given them. A terrible burning was in her throat and a harsh wrenching noise came from deep inside her. And then Lally, the girl who shared her berth, was up and holding her forehead, gagging as she did it.

"How long?" Nory asked when she could speak.

"Forty days," Lally said. "Maybe even longer."

Nory closed her eyes. Forty days was more than she could count.

Enough to eat, a place to sleep. The rocking of the ship that made the passengers and even a few of the sailors ill didn't bother Sean at all.

He was used to the sea, to his brother's currach. He remembered the roll of the waves, higher than any house in Maidin Bay, the rush of salt water slapping against the sturdy boat.

Once he had even been swept out and under just outside the bay. He had opened his eyes to see a green world filled with bubbles, and then light as he came to the surface, gulping and choking, and felt Francey's fingers grasping him first by the hair and then by the sleeve of his jersey to drag him up and up and finally into the currach.

He'd had a bald spot on his head all that fall, and

Nory had teased him that he looked better without that mop of red hair.

Nory.

If only he could tell her about the things that had happened to him.

He worked from halfway through one night until late the following night. He remembered Mam saying, *"I work from dark to dark."* He could almost see her, hands on her hips, angry. But he couldn't even see the dark, couldn't see the day.

He was in the galley with only the flame from the lamps to brighten it, or in the passageway to bring tea to the families that were rich enough to have their own cabin. It was Garvey who went up on top and told him when the sun was shining or the rain spitting.

What Sean did was stir pots of soup for those rich families who had shoes and rings, unlike the poor wretches that he caught glimpses of between the decks. There were two different worlds on the ship, almost like the green world of water he had seen against the clear world of air up above.

The pots he stirred were never empty; they were filled with shreds of meat, and old vegetables still covered with some of the gritty soil they'd been taken from, and water they kept adding to the top.

He dipped endless ladles into those pots to pour into thick white bowls and then brought them to rich men's cabins. Sometimes he and Garvey dipped their fingers into the soup to pull out a small chunk of yellow turnip as it floated by, or a cabbage leaf. Their fingers had blisters, but it was worth it to have their stomachs filled, as long as the cook didn't see what they had done.

The cook was a massive man who ate more than six passengers put together, and chewed endlessly with his great toothless mouth open and soup running down his beard. He threw knives and plates, and kicked and punched at anyone nearby when he was angry.

Sean felt a sharp clout on the back of his head. "You can dream with the fishes," the cook said. "I'll send you up top with the garbage to be thrown overboard."

Sean bent his head. "Yes, sir." He wondered if the cook could do such a thing; he shuddered as he thought of that green world and the blackness underneath as he was pulled down into it.

Quickly he filled bowls with tea, black as the tar on their old currach. He darted around the cook as he took three of the bowls on a tray and left the galley to bring them to the book cabin. He called it that because the man who stayed there with his wife and daughter was always bent over a huge book, mumbling and nodding, and next to him was a young girl who had a book of her own. Younger than he was, eight maybe, and she could read.

The woman was still sick when he knocked at the door. The room smelled of vomit, and she shook her head wearily. "No tea," she said in English. "I can't look at it."

Sean thought there was something wrong with the woman anyway. A walking stick was propped up near her bunk.

But the little girl wasn't sick. Sean couldn't imagine her sick. She looked up from her book, curling a piece of her hair around her fingers. "Tea," she said, looking down at his bare feet.

The man held out one hand for his bowl, still reading, and Sean went toward him to stand there, looking down at that book covered in the softest material with letters running across the page.

Just then the ship lurched and the tray of tea bowls slid. Sean caught them just in time, leaning into the man, but as he looked down he saw that a drop of tea had splashed on the page.

The man saw it too. He looked up at Sean, blinking, almost surprised to see him there. Then he rubbed his sleeve across the page, blotting the mark, which had spread into a line covering some of the letters.

"I'm sorry." How angry he would have been if it had been his. And could the cook send him into the green water that tilted just beyond a tiny round window in the man's cabin?

*Thrown overboard with the garbage.*

"I'm really sorry," he said, almost stuttering.

The man looked up at him, his eyes large in back of eyeglasses. "You've covered King Herod with tea," he said. The sound of his voice was different, almost like Lord Cunningham's in Maidin Bay. English.

"King Herod," the man said again. "A terrible ruler from the biblical days."

"I don't understand," Sean began, and remembered quickly to add "Your honor."

The man ran his finger over the damp page. "See it? Herod."

Sean could hardly breathe. He did see it. It jumped off the page at him. The *H* of it, the *D* at the end. And then he did something he couldn't believe. He reached out and touched the word: *Herod.*

"If you look beyond it," the man said, "you'll see the word *King.*"

Sean nodded, then backed away from him, still holding the tray, and went into the hallway. It wasn't until he reached the galley that he realized he had forgotten to give the man his tea.

He thought about going back, but he couldn't do that either. He'd take the chance that the man had forgotten too.

And he knew those two words, *King* and *Herod.* He'd never forget them, never. And when he brought the tea next time, maybe he'd see another word.

He wondered if Herod was an Englishman.

And then he thought of Patch and his mam, and Nory still back in Maidin Bay. What would they think if they knew how happy he had been for a moment?

# FIFTEEN

## NORY

Nory lay on the straw mattress, her nose and cheek pressed against the rough wood of the berth, while above her a lamp swung on its hook, the flame so low it gave almost no light. But even that tiny bit of light was better than nothing. Most of the time the ship bobbed so much that they weren't allowed any light, and the cabin was completely dark.

She ran her hand over her stomach. Some of the others were still sick, but she was better now, much better, and Patch hadn't been sick at all.

Nearby a baby was crying. In the dim light Nory could see the mother holding the little one. Bits of cloth were strung on a string over their heads. Filthy cloths for the baby.

*Fuafar.*

The woman must have seen her looking at the

cloths. "There is no place to wash them," she called across the berths. "I can only let them dry and put them on her again."

Nory shook her head.

"There's not enough water," the woman said, rocking the screaming baby, "and if I use salt water it will burn her. My poor baby. My poor Bridgie."

Nory leaned back. She had a memory of Patch as a baby, shrieking for Mam. Poor baby. Mam had died just after he was born. She remembered Maggie dipping her finger into a precious bit of sugar and then into Patch's mouth. He had closed his eyes then, at last asleep.

She looked down at Patch, his eyes closed now too, his thumb in his mouth. She ran her hand over his soft hair and pulled Lally's old coat up over his thin shoulders.

Suddenly the baby stopped crying, and everything seemed still for just that moment. But almost immediately came the sound of coughing, and Granda talking to Mr. Casey in the berth above, and a woman calling for her husband, and someone else being sick. And above it all was the endless roll of the ship with the timbers creaking and the planks groaning as it plowed its way through the ocean.

In the midst of all those other noises was a voice she had heard before, a voice that cried out in pain. It took her a moment of thinking. Who was it?

And then she realized. It was the girl with the plank, the girl who had stolen the money, she was sure of it.

She sat up in the bunk and rolled over Lally, hesitating. She hated to put her feet on that bare floor. During the night someone nearby had been sick. She made sure the cut on her foot was covered as she stepped onto the slippery wood.

Around her were bunks, one after another, so close she could have held out one arm to touch the person in the next.

Where was that girl?

The motion of the ship was stronger now, and the wooden plates of the deck under her feet shifted with each wave, separating, then joining together again. One of the plates opened under her slightly and just as quickly shut again, catching her skirt in its grip.

She reached out to catch her balance on the edge of the nearest berth, then bent over to yank at the bottom of her skirt. It didn't give. But just then a wave, fiercer than she had felt before, smashed into the side of the ship.

Her skirt came free as the plate of the floor opened again with a faint whoosh. She pulled it up around her ankles and stood there holding an upright bar, peering through the dim cabin to see if she could find the girl.

At that moment the hatch was opened and a beam of light played against the wall. The steward, his head upside down over her head, called, "Cookstoves lighted. Fight over them and the captain will make me close the hatch again." His voice sounded stern, but it was Garvey, the friendly man she had called *your honor.*

Nory went back to help Patch climb down from the bunk, and then Granda, too, from above her.

"Go ahead," she told them, feeling the hunger in her stomach. "I just want to . . ." Her voice trailed off. Wanted to find the girl, that was what she wanted to do. The thief with the dark curly hair who had stolen her food, stolen money from the ticket seller, but had found that plank of wood for her.

Patch and Granda climbed the steps, wooden bowls from Mrs. Casey in their hands. "I'll bring you stirabout," Patch called down to her. "I'll give you the most."

She blew him a kiss, still watching for the girl. Even with twenty people gone up on top, there were so many people in that space.

But again she heard the cry of pain, and at last she saw her, a swirl of dark hair under an old coat. Probably a stolen coat, she thought.

She reached for the girl's shoulder and watched her turn. Even in that small bit of light she could see that the girl's face was dark with a yellow cast, and she was moaning still.

Yellow. What had Anna called that?

"Do you know who I am?" Nory asked, but the girl's eyes were glazed, the whites of them as yellow as her skin.

Nory sat on the very edge of the straw watching as the girl's eyes closed again.

What would Anna have done?

She remembered that dark disease, and Anna had told her the patients always died, faces black and bloated. But there was another sickness where the skin was more yellow than black. Nory leaned forward. Wasn't the girl's face more yellow than dark? She had the seeds for that, safe in her bag on the very inside of her bunk. Buttercups, dried and waiting to be boiled.

Boiled on the makeshift stove on the foredeck.

Nory pulled the coat up higher over the girl. "Wait," she said.

She went toward the stairs, but there was a ragged line in front of her. "Please," she said, trying to push through.

Someone pushed back, but she had her foot on the step and managed to climb, pushing away the hand that reached out to grab her sleeve. "I need help," she said.

"We all need help," someone answered bitterly.

She almost fell, but Garvey looked down on them from above. "Let the girl up," he said.

Then she was on the deck, blinking in the light, thanking him. "Someone is sick," she told him, "and I need to boil water for buttercups."

"Yes, your honor," he said, smiling at her. "But you'll not find buttercups here, with the sea spread out in every direction."

"I have the buttercups. It's a cure," she said, wondering if it really was.

She begged a place in the line ahead of Granda and waited to boil water for the girl.

# SIXTEEN

## SEAN

He awoke to the rolling of the ship, to the rough bulkhead he slept against, remembering he had dreamed of yellow flowers. He thought now of the castle ruins outside of Ballilee. On warm summer days the fields were filled with the small flowers. It seemed right to him that a castle would have that gold and silver: buttercups against the sparkle of stone.

Garvey had been telling him a story about buttercups. Someone had cured a young girl who had been ill with the yellow sickness.

"A pert thing, that healer," he had said. "Every morning she pushed her way up out of the hold against a dozen bigger and stronger than she was. Boiled water and mixed it with the dried buttercups." Garvey's thin face had broken into a smile as he slapped Sean's back. "Called me *your honor* once."

Sean remembered Anna who cured. Anna had a wrinkled face and knobby hands, and leaves and powders. She was teaching Nory all about them.

Thinking about Anna reminded him of Mam and Patch and gave him a terrible burning in his chest. What he thought about, what he couldn't stop thinking about, was the book cabin and the Englishman bent over that huge book. What would it be like to hold the book in his own hands, to find the two words he had seen, and to look for a third word and a fourth?

From his place in the corner under a shelf he suddenly realized that everything had come to life. The cook was sharpening his knife against a leather strap with a great swishing sound as his small gray eyes swept across the galley. Garvey, legs spread for balance, stood in front of a heap of turnips, rubbing his eyes and yawning. Someone else stirred the endless soup.

Sean scrambled up, sliding out from under the table in back of the cook. But the cook turned quickly on his thick legs. "Sleeping all day?"

Sean saw the flash of silver and ducked away as the knife punctured the wood of the bulkhead over his head and hung there. He didn't move fast enough to miss the cook's meaty hand as it came around to hit the side of his head.

There was a quick throb of pain, then a distant ringing in his ear, but he managed to mutter something about the Englishman's tea. "I'll take it to him now." He wanted to raise his hand to his ear but wiped his hands on his jersey instead.

He darted away to fill the bowls and escaped to the passageway. For a moment he stood there holding the tray with one hand as he touched the side of his ear and felt the wetness of blood. Then he knocked at the cabin door. All was quiet and he began to think no one was inside.

He reached for the knob, beginning to feel his heart thump. Perhaps they were on the deck; perhaps it was a fine morning. He remembered late spring mornings in Maidin Bay when the sky was filled with a rosy color as the sun lifted over the land in back of them.

There was no one in the room, and the woman's walking stick was gone. He slid the tray onto the berth, glanced at the shelf where the book lay, and then quickly looked back at the door. His hands felt as clammy as they had when he used to gut fish for Liam.

What would happen if he touched the book? They would think he was a thief. He would be beaten, he was sure of that, and perhaps the cook really would throw him overboard. And who would know if the cook dragged him up to the deck at night?

But still he reached out and ran his fingers over the soft leather on the back of the book. Almost without thinking he pulled it toward him and opened it.

There were too many pages to find the words he knew, he could see that almost immediately, but he looked for the letters in those words, and the letters of his own name.

"What are you doing?" a voice said.

Sean spun around, almost dropping the heavy book, felt his heart reach up into his throat. He hadn't even heard the cabin door open.

It was the girl. His mouth was suddenly so dry he couldn't say anything. He looked at the door in back of her, but it seemed so far away that he couldn't imagine taking those few steps around her to escape back into the hallway.

"You can't read that book," she said in English.

"I was just . . . ," he began, hearing his voice, which didn't even sound like his own.

"You can't read at all, I think." She took a step forward. "How can that be?"

He noticed that her cheeks were red and her curls twisted. She reminded him of Nory when Nory was eight or maybe nine. "I know the letters," he said slowly, thinking that she would surely tell her father. But if she didn't, if by some miracle he managed to get out of that cabin, he'd never go back in there again. He'd ask Garvey to bring the tea for him instead.

She pushed at her hair. "It's windy outside," she said. "My mother is afraid of it, but I like to look at the water. It bunches up and up, and just when it seems as if it will go over the ship it flattens out again."

She walked around him now and it seemed as if he'd be able to escape, but she picked up her own book. "It's called *Aesop's Fables*," she said. "I could teach you some of the words."

He shook his head again, looking back at the door. "That's all right."

She waved her hand. "No one will mind."

He thought about the door just a few feet away, but she was waving the book at him. "Look at the cover," she said. "Aesop is the name of the man who told the fables. They're all about animals: foxes and crows and cranes and wolves. The foxes and wolves are always bad."

He took a step forward as she opened the book and began to read, running her fingers under the lines. She read in a loud voice, sometimes stumbling a bit over the words.

He was caught up in the story of a fox who was trying to get a piece of cheese away from a mouse. He saw the letters of the fox turn into a word, and the ones for mouse and cheese as well. And then that first story was finished and she began to read one about a wolf who was chasing a lamb.

Sean watched as she read that story, trying to grab on to the words. Then suddenly he remembered. The cook would be waiting. How long had he been gone? He could feel the rush of fear in his throat again.

"I must go," he said, backing toward the door.

He backed away from her, then opened the door and went out into the passageway.

He turned and there was the cook, blocking the way.

The girl lay in the berth, her heavy hair covering her face. Nory swept it back, and the girl reached up in her fever to tangle her fingers in the long strands of it. At last Mrs. Casey came with a scissors. A scissors! Anna kept a small one on her table, but there had never been one in Nory's house. Together they snipped the long hair so the girl would be more comfortable.

Later they found that her name was Eliza. And from the first time Nory mixed the dried flowers into the boiled water and fed it to her from the small cracked cup, she became stronger. By the tenth day she was on her feet, weak, tottering, her face the color of cheese from Mrs. Mallon's goat, but alive.

That morning she held on to Nory's sleeve, raising her eyes to the hatch cover as it opened. "Help me up," she said. "Help me out."

Nory looked doubtfully at the steps, which were already lined with people. They held pots and cups and small pans to fill with meal as Garvey doled it out to them.

So many people! Sometimes she remembered running along the cliff path in Maidin Bay, arms stretched out as far as they could go, feeling the mist on her head and her shoulders. But here on the ship, even on the deck, there was no room to spin or even to turn without bumping into someone or stepping on someone's bare toes. She was never alone. Everywhere she turned someone was talking, or sleeping, or fighting, or sick.

She turned to Eliza. "Maybe you'd better stay in your berth. Let me get food."

But Eliza was moving toward the steps. Nory hesitated, looking toward Granda's bunk, and in the dim light she could see he was still asleep, and Patch too, in the filthy straw on the berth beneath.

In Brooklyn everything would be clean, she thought. Clean straw smelling of sunny fields, clothes washed, hands washed, faces washed.

She took Granda's bowl and stood in line with Eliza as they climbed onto the deck. There was a strange cast to the sky this morning, and after Garvey filled her bowl with a cup of meal she found a small empty place out of the wind for the two of them to sit while they waited to use the makeshift stove.

A fierce red ball of sun had hurled itself over the horizon, and she squinted uneasily at it and that greenish light in the distance.

Eliza's head was back, her eyes closed. "You saved

my life. I'm not sorry I left you the rest of your food when we were on the road."

"I wouldn't have let you take it," Nory said, smiling because they both knew she couldn't have stopped her.

Eliza opened her eyes. "I am here because of an apple."

Nory shook her head. "I don't understand."

"I climbed the wall of the squire's garden," she said. "One apple hung there, the only one. It had held on all winter, green and hard, and I had the feel of it in my mouth. Every morning I passed under the wall and the tree and that apple holding on to it, and I thought if I could just put my teeth into it, I wouldn't care what happened afterward."

Nory could feel the taste of it in her own mouth. She remembered Anna finding them an apple last winter. She and Patch had eaten it, skin, pulp, even the core.

She looked down at the meal in her cup. The grains shifted almost like the sand at the base of the cliffs when it was invaded by tiny summer fleas. The meal was filled with insects.

She thought about the meal Maggie would have for them in Brooklyn, golden grain she could run her fingers through, clean and clear and softened in pure water.

Eliza was still talking in that harsh voice. "I wasn't strong enough to put my feet in the chinks of the wall to climb it, but one day the iron gate was open and I slid inside."

She and Sean had done that, Nory remembered, feeling the ache of wondering what had happened to him.

"I took the apple," Eliza said. "I climbed the tree on

the squire's side of the wall, and I saw his children. Fat. Can you imagine that? They had food, all the food they wanted, and I had to steal a winter apple."

Nory didn't answer. She patted Eliza's arm absently as she looked up. She had seen a sky like that before, shot through with green, but she couldn't remember when.

"I picked up a stone," Eliza said.

Nory turned. "You threw it at the children?"

"At the window. At the great square window." Eliza's eyes were closed again. "I can hear the sound of it, the glass shattering, a piece left in one corner. Someone came after me, and I ran, just ran."

Nory sighed. She could almost tell the rest of the story herself. Eliza had not gone home again. If she had, the rest of her family would have been out on the road, their house tumbled.

"There were eight of us at home," Eliza said, "and I'm thinking I won't see any of them again but my brother Owen in America." She shook herself. "There's a storm somewhere."

*That's what it is,* Nory thought. A storm in the distance. Around them the sea seemed peaceful enough; the swells were large, but they were smooth. There were no crashing waves, no great white arcs to the water.

"A bad storm," Eliza said, her eyes opening now. "But it will stay far away if we have luck."

Somewhere on the ocean, Nory thought, far to the west, or was it to the south?

And in her memory . . .

The door to their small house rattling, rattling, blowing open, no rain, but the sky! That terrible sky. Mam trying to hold the door against the wind. Sean

Red's father far out in the bay fishing and Mrs. Mallon standing on the hill, hands pulling at her skirt. Da looking up at the sky. "If the storm doesn't turn, Mallon will never survive." And the rain had come then, and Mr. Mallon and his small boat had disappeared.

"I've seen a sky like that before," Nory said, trying to find comfort in Eliza's words: *"Maybe it will stay far away."*

She shaded her eyes, looking toward the horizon. Da and Celia were on a ship somewhere ahead of them. Surely they hadn't reached Brooklyn yet. Was the storm threatening them?

She could feel the ship rising, rising, then settling back again. Nory shivered. Underneath that great rolling mass were giant shadowy fish that swam silently in the darkness, and hulls of sunken ships that held skeleton sailors with their bony arms outstretched.

Garvey shook his head at the horizon too, reaching for the water pail. "Have to douse the fire in the stoves," he said.

"Wait," the next person in line called, and in a moment people were pushing Garvey away from the stoves, so many people that Nory could hardly see him in the midst of them. Two sailors came, pushing and shoving too, and one man was thrown down the steps into the hold. Others lost their balance and slid down on top of him. Those who were left still tried to get the last bit of heat from the stove as Garvey poured the water over it and wisps of steam rose into the air.

A jagged streak of lightning shot across the sky, and Eliza nodded. "It might be that it will take the ship."

"Don't say that," Nory told her.

"If it isn't the storm," Eliza said, "it will be something else."

They climbed down into the hold listening to the moans of the man who had fallen, and went to Nory's berth. Patch was sitting on the edge, his legs crossed under him. "Do you remember potatoes?" he said. "Do you remember Maggie boiled them for us?"

*Maggie with the rush pot filled with potatoes, the boiling water spilling out the bottom on the doorstep.*

Nory took a breath.

*The day the potatoes failed. Every field in Maidin Bay covered with oozing plants, that terrible smell.*

Nory reached out to give Patch the meal that she had softened with water. "There will be potatoes in Brooklyn, fine white ones," she said. "But in the meantime I will take this meal and stir it with water even though it won't be warm." She tried to sound cheerful.

Eliza moved Patch's feet out of the way and sat on a corner of the bunk. Lally, lying there, whispered, "No room," and was back to sleep in an instant.

Eliza ran her fingers through the faded little ribbon she wore around her neck. Nory smiled, remembering that she had had a ribbon like that once, remembered Sean chasing her on the cliff top, and heard an echo of the words Eliza had said about her family: *"I'm thinking I won't see any of them again."*

She'd never see Sean again either.

Nory raised her hand as Eliza stared back at her, both of them realizing there had been a change in the movement of the ship. Instead of plowing straight through the water, the force of the waves pulled it to the side.

Nory thought about Sean's brother Liam in his open

fishing boat. *"The thing of it is, Nory, to keep her straight into the waves. She'll want to turn, but if you let that happen, she'll be hit by one of those waves and roll over."*

"People are going to die," Eliza said.

Nory glanced at Patch, his thumb in his mouth, his large eyes staring. "Don't," she said, angry that Eliza would frighten him.

"Look around you," Eliza said. "It's not only the storm, although I think we're in for it, but there will be fever. No air, no food, and people are coughing." She lowered her voice, leaning forward, pointing. "They are coughing out bad spirits that swirl around us. I can feel them. They call it ship fever."

Nory took a breath. "That is not true." If only she had salt, though, even a grain to throw over her shoulder, she wouldn't have been so uneasy.

Eliza took a strand of Patch's hair and ran it through her fingers. "Your granda with the white beard. There's nothing left of him."

Patch pulled away from her. "We'll start a farm in Brooklyn. Granda has said so. We'll build a barn as big as Lord Cunningham's. There will be sheep, and a cow." He looked up. "Isn't that right? And I'll name the cow Biddy after our poor old hen."

But all the while Patch was talking, Nory was thinking about Granda. The skin between his shoulder bones was so sunken she could put her fingers deep inside those hollows. And yesterday when they had been up on deck, she had seen how gray he looked, how dull his blue eyes were.

He had looked over the sea that rolled and tilted.

"When I was young," he'd told Nory, "I sailed this sea, but I knew at the end of the voyage I'd be sailing east to Ireland, not west to a strange land."

They had gone to a fair long ago in Ballilee. Someone had played a fiddle, a rollicking song that made her feet tap. Granda had lifted her high into the air, dancing with her to the music so her legs swung out, and when they stopped finally, breathless, people clapped and asked for more. And so they had danced once more, Granda patting her shoulder and telling her how much she looked like her mam.

Was that the same Granda who stayed in his bunk all day, his thin coat draped over him? How could that be?

"Are you all right then, Granda?" she called suddenly.

"It's just a small nap I'm taking," he answered.

"We will build a barn, won't we?" Patch said.

"A barn with piles of new hay," Granda began, but he wasn't able to finish.

They never felt the wave, just the roll of the ship that seemed to go on forever. Boxes and crates shifted; something split open with a wrenching sound. And then the ship righted itself only to begin another roll, turning deeper and deeper into the sea.

Nory was tossed out of her bunk with Patch and Eliza in back of her, and Granda from overhead. It was as if everyone's mouth opened at once in one long scream.

## EIGHTEEN

### SEAN

With the first wild crosscut of the sea, there was frenzy in the galley with the cook shouting orders to them and sweeping things off the table into drawers below.

Between the smash of the waves that sent them sliding on their backs from bulkhead to table, Sean and Garvey managed to douse the fires under the huge pots of soup. Another roll and they lashed the leather straps across the cabinet doors over the bags of meal, the tea, the nests of bowls, and the cook's knives.

Before the third, they slammed down bin tops over thick turnips. A cabinet door opened again, as though it had a life of its own, and Sean pushed against it, pushed hard to close it.

The cook, wild-eyed, rolled into his great trundle bed muttering to himself. Sean and Garvey were left to fend for themselves. Sean could imagine what it was like to drown. Hadn't he seen that green world under the surface of the sea? Hadn't he felt himself choking in that terrible water?

But this time it seemed worse, so much worse. He'd be trapped deep inside the ship as the water rose; he'd scramble to find air to breathe where there was none. At least if he was outside on the deck, he'd have a chance to float to the top, catch a few gulps of air, find something to hang on to.

Garvey must have been thinking the same thing. He pointed and they scrambled out of the galley into the cabin hallway. Ahead of them was the book man's cabin, the cabin the cook had told him he was never to set foot in again.

Just the thought of the cook blocking his way last week was enough to send a thin thread of fear running through him.

The cook had clenched his hand on Sean's shoulder, squeezing so tightly Sean felt as if his bones were being crushed.

"What were you doing in there?" The cook's face had been so close Sean could see the smear of food across his mouth. "Answer me."

But even if he had wanted to say something, the pain was so great he was unable to open his mouth.

"Stay out of there." The cook had shoved him against the bulkhead. "If I see you in that room again, it will be the end of you."

Now Sean rushed down that passageway in back of Garvey, his arms out to steady himself, his bare feet slipping on the wet floor, seeing tiny rivulets of water running along the floorboards. All he could think about now was to reach the outside where he could breathe, where he wouldn't be trapped.

The stairway was just ahead of him. Garvey was reaching for the handrail, already climbing, as Sean passed the book man's cabin. The door swung open wildly.

Inside, the book man's wife was huddled in her bunk, eyes wide, terrified. "Boy," she called. "Help me."

Sean looked toward the stairway where Garvey had disappeared, then back toward the galley, where one of the soup pots had escaped from its strap and was clattering across the floor.

"Please," the woman called.

Now Sean held on to the edge of the doorway, wondering where the book man was.

"My husband is searching for Elizabeth," the woman said. "We can't find her anywhere."

*Elizabeth*, he thought. The girl's name was Elizabeth.

Directly across from him, the porthole was green with the froth of water, covered with it, and as the ship righted itself, the water disappeared, and a circle of sky appeared with a strange yellow color.

"She could not have gone into the galley," he said. "I would have seen her."

"Find her, please."

He nodded at the woman and ran down the passageway past the galley, thinking about being deep inside the ship when the next roll might turn it over. Still he kept going through the small maze where the passageway was so narrow there was room for only one person. And she wasn't there. She might be anywhere.

He felt dizzy from the motion of the ship, and when he went back again past the galley, the cabinets were banging open, cups and saucers were in dozens of pieces, bags of flour torn open and mixed with soup and water.

And then he remembered that the girl had said how much she liked the look of the waves. He went toward the ladder and climbed as Garvey had done, feeling the railing tilt under his fingers, but smelling the difference in the air, the freshness of it, the cold of it.

Rope had been slung across the deck and he held on as he inched his way across in the drenching rain. He could see sailors climbing the mast but Garvey was nowhere in sight. It took another moment to see the girl huddled against the railing, holding on to the rope, and he went toward her calling, "Elizabeth!"

He led her back to her cabin, her mother reaching out to her as he backed away and went down the passageway to the galley.

# NINETEEN
## NORY

At last it was quiet in the dark hold. Mrs. Casey's pig squealed once and was still. They were past those terrible waves, and Nory pictured them crashing across the ocean to beat themselves out on the cliffs of Maidin Bay. Poor *Samson* had stopped that terrible groaning noise, but others around her made up for it: People all around her were crying.

Mrs. Casey slid out of the bunk above her. "My poor piglet is gone," she said. "He's nothing now but a wee gray lump in his bag. He must have been caught beneath us in the berth and crushed."

Nory shook her head. She remembered her own pig, Muc, rubbing her sides against the pen, eyes turned up to her as if she were a thin old woman herself. *Ah, Muc.*

"Isn't it strange?" Mrs. Casey said. "I've lost almost everything I've loved. My house, the bed on a stand my

117

father made for us, the sight of the mountain with its wreath of mist in the morning, and I never once cried. But now I can't seem to stop."

Nory bit her lip. It was hard to know what to say. But before she could open her mouth, Mrs. Casey drew herself up. "I'll go up on top and give my piglet a decent sea burial. At least the landlord never had him to himself."

"What is it?" Patch asked, his head popping up from under a coat on the bunk. "Who is going to be buried?"

"It's nothing," Nory said, waiting until Mrs. Casey had climbed the stairway and disappeared in back of a knot of people. "Now, Patch. Would you like to go up to the far side of the deck? We will see the sunshine at last, and cook a wee cup of oats just for you."

Patch slid out of the bunk. She could see he was dizzy. She felt dizzy herself. It was strange to feel the deck under her, steady again.

She raised her head. "Granda, come with us."

He didn't answer, but she could hear him coughing. She called again.

"I will just stay here for a while," he said, "and sleep now that it's calm."

Up on deck Nory waited in line for her chance at the stove. Eliza slept too, she told herself, rolled into the smallest ball in her berth with two other women. It didn't mean anything that Granda was not up and about.

Still she was uneasy, and during the day she kept calling up, "Are you all right, Granda?" She tried to tell herself that she had the cures if he needed them, bags of dried foxglove, packets of marigold; she would keep him alive no matter what.

In the middle of the night Mrs. Casey plucked at Nory's sleeve. "The old man is having trouble breathing."

Nory reached for her bag, fingers trembling, fumbling, searching for Anna's packets of leaves and flowers, Anna's weeds, spilling a few in her haste.

What would Anna have done?

She didn't even know what was happening to Granda. Was it the spirits Eliza had spoken of?

Mrs. Casey stood next to the bunk, the light of the flame from the lamp reflected in her eyes. She put her hand on Nory's shoulder. "I think it may be his time," she said slowly.

"How can you say that?" Nory looked at her fiercely. "We have come so far. He must get to Maggie's. We must be together again, all of us: Maggie, and Da, and Celia." She could hardly get the words out. "Patch. And Granda."

Mrs. Casey reached out to her. "You are young, you will start over," she said. "America will be your country. But for the old people, for your old granda, to leave the country he loved and begin again . . ." Her voice trailed off.

Nory pulled away from Mrs. Casey. She had the cure for him right in her hands, those small cloth bags filled with seeds and leaves Anna had gathered for her for just this purpose.

Mr. Casey came down from the top berth and stood with Mrs. Casey, running his hand over his sparse beard. "Go up to him," he said.

Nory climbed up to see Granda lying on his side. She

could hear his breathing now, in and out, and then it stopped . . . and began again.

She crouched over, feeling the bags with her fingers. Moss for wounds, bark of the barberry for stomach ailments; dandelion was there too, and dried garlic.

And even more than the bags were the other things she had learned from Anna: ashes to cover chicken pox, the smoke from a hot coal to stop sneezing.

She reached for his shoulder. "Tell me," she whispered. "What hurts you?"

He turned slightly. "Maggie?"

"No, it's Nory."

"Ah, Nory," he said, and the words were nothing more than a breath.

"What is it?" She put her hand on his forehead and could feel the heat. So fever, then. The only thing she could think of for that was food. And there wouldn't be any until morning.

Still she mixed leaves from one bag with dried flowers from another and added precious drops of water that Mrs. Casey gave her from a small bottle. She spooned the mixture into his mouth, drop by drop, during the rest of the night. Then, feeling her legs trembling underneath her, her eyes drooping, she went up on deck in the morning to beg hot water from Garvey.

She slept in snatches that day and the next, trying first one of Anna's cures and then another. Nothing helped. She'd drift off, her head jerking, holding Granda's hand in hers, hardly paying attention to Patch as he told her about the farm they'd have: "Cows and hens, Nory. Tell that to Granda. Tell him not to forget.

There will be a stream. It will have a great salmon that will swim up to see us."

And Eliza's voice in her head: *"Bad spirits that swirl around us."*

Why, Nory wondered, had Anna's cures worked when Eliza was sick, and why were they not working for Granda?

Sometimes she'd doze off and Anna's face would float in front of hers. Anna's dear face. How had she ever thought she could cure the way Anna had?

On the morning of the third day Granda turned his head slightly toward her. "I must go home."

It reminded her of Mrs. Mallon. Wasn't that what she had said? Had Mrs. Mallon reached Maidin Bay? Was she with Anna or had she died on the road? How terrible, Mrs. Mallon dead. She thought about Sean and never seeing either of them again.

"I must go home," he whispered again.

"We are on the ship," she said carefully. "The *Samson*, remember?"

His fingers plucked at the coat that covered his shoulders. "If I go too far, I will never go back," he said.

He was raving, she thought, not knowing what he was saying. "Take a little water," she said. "I have put in leaves for your throat."

But then with a slight movement of his head she could see his eyes. She saw that he knew her, but she had to lean close to hear him.

"You have been a great girl always," he said. "You will get Patch to New York."

"Oh, Granda." She took his hand. It was cold, really

cold. How could it be with the fever of his head? She had to have something to give him; she had to remember all the things Anna had told her. But it was hard to think. And he was speaking again.

"You will think of me in Maidin Bay," he said, giving her hand the slightest squeeze. "Will you do that?"

It was the last thing he said. A few hours later, when Garvey pulled the hatch cover away, letting light beam down onto them, she saw that he had stopped breathing.

She rocked back and forth on the edge of the bunk, hearing a strange sound coming from her own throat. Keening, Mrs. Casey called it, holding Nory to her.

How could she ever tell Maggie? How could she tell any of them that she hadn't saved him?

At last they all helped, wrapping Granda in his coat, Mrs. Casey combing his soft white beard. He would be buried there in the sea, Nory told herself, but his soul would be on its way to Maidin Bay. He'd see the cliffs again, and their wee house. He'd find Bird, the grandmother she had never met.

Later in the day she took the small cloth bags that held all of Anna's cures and tossed them over the side of the ship. They bobbed on the water and then at last they were gone. She'd never think about cures again.

# TWENTY

## SEAN

It took days to get the galley right again. In between chopping and cutting and stirring the soup Sean spent the time down on his hands and knees. He picked up broken cups and plates; he swept the piles of powdery flour and lumpy meal into a bin. The cook was raging: He sent more crockery across the galley to smash against the bulkhead, spoons and pieces of biscuit following. He dug his knife into the great wooden table and clenched his filthy apron with huge hands.

Sean never raised his head. He had seen a turtle on the strand once, its head deep inside its shell for safety. He had knelt on the sand looking into the turtle's eyes, then helped Francey turn it back to the sea. He felt the same way now as the turtle must have felt, wanting to bury his head in his neck. How had he ever come to be here on this ship, in this galley, when he should have been home working the lazy beds for potato planting, or standing on the misty cliff top with Nory, the wind whistling around them?

He looked toward the place where he slept. It was a narrow spot under a shelf, and he wished he could curl up there under his old coat.

At last the cleanup after the storm was finished. He mopped the galley as the cook sank down in his trundle bed, his eyes closed.

Now Sean could leave the galley; he might even go up on deck. He had been there only twice during the whole journey, once during the storm and once at night when stars coated the sky all the way to the horizon.

Where he wanted to go, he could not go. He wanted to walk along the passageway to that cabin and look at the girl's book with its stories of wolves and lambs and foxes. He wanted to learn a word, learn a page.

But the cook never slept for long. He'd take a few minutes here, a few there, like the cat they'd had once in Maidin Bay. And when Sean least expected it, those cruel eyes would be on him, that great mouth open to yell vile things.

But now the cook gave him a pitcher of a foul-smelling drink. "Go up onto the deck," he said. "Give this to Garvey. He forgot to take it with him for the captain."

Sean took a quick look. Was Garvey in trouble? If something set the cook off against one of them, the other would be in for trouble as well. But the cook turned away without saying anything more.

Sean went past the man's cabin quickly, but even so he could see the woman sitting on the edge of her bunk with a bit of sewing and Elizabeth bent over her book. Neither of them looked up and he hurried past.

He stood on the deck at the top of the ladder. The sea was glass smooth and he remembered days when he had been home with all his brothers, Francey and Liam and Michael, out in the bay when they could see the bowl of it surrounded by the cliffs. He wondered where Liam and Michael were, fishing somewhere out on the ocean. Maybe someday they'd travel to the shore of America too, in one of their ships. He looked out at the water, able to see so far, it seemed he could look back to Ireland and forward to America.

For that moment Sean was happy to see the light that played across the water, to glance up and see a sky so blue it hurt his eyes. The sun warmed his face so his skin and hair felt dry instead of wet and cold, and he could almost feel the dampness leaving his clothing.

Brooklyn would be like this, he was sure of it, with a bright sun throwing shadows across the land or a soft rain that would green up the meadows.

The man was on the deck. Sean saw him. Had Elizabeth told him about the book? He went quickly toward Garvey with the pitcher in his hand.

Garvey was at the fireboxes with a line of people in front of him. "Oh, lad," he said. "You're up in the daylight."

"Only for this one thing," Sean said. "You are to give this pitcher to the captain."

They stared at each other. "I've forgotten it today," Garvey said, his eyes worried.

Sean went back to the ladder, moving quickly now

because the cook might be waiting, judging how long it took him.

He felt the hand on his shoulder then, and jumped away, feeling his heart pound up into his throat.

The book man.

"I didn't mean to frighten you," he said.

Sean could hardly look up at him.

"You found Elizabeth," the man said. "I thank you for that."

Only that. Not the book at all. Just bringing Elizabeth back to the cabin in the storm. He shrugged a little to let the man know he was glad to have done it.

"She might have been swept away," the man said.

"It's all right." Sean took a breath, thinking of the cook in his trundle bed, asleep but not asleep, waiting to pounce on him.

He went past the man and back toward the galley, and this time Elizabeth looked up as he passed and called to him.

He wouldn't have gone into the room, but the mother wasn't there and the book was in Elizabeth's hand, and so, just for a minute, he told himself, he'd go in and look at the book once more.

It wasn't until later, much later, that he was aware of how much time had gone by. He backed away from Elizabeth and put his hand on the cabin door, almost afraid to open it.

# TWENTY-ONE

## NORY

She sat on the deck in a place out of the wind, her head back against the bulkhead.

"Stay there," Eliza had said. "I'll take care of the little one."

Before she wouldn't have trusted Patch with Eliza, but now all she wanted to do was to sleep or to sit somewhere doing nothing, thinking nothing.

She glanced at the people around her. She made herself concentrate on them. So many of them. Some were leaning the railing. One man had a long string. He had attached a shirt to it and dangled it far over the side of the ship. Washing his clothes, she told herself.

Children were everywhere, chasing each other, running around knots of women who leaned together, talking.

After a while she closed her eyes. On such a day,

with the sun warm on her eyelids, it was hard to imagine the terrible storm they'd been through. It was hard to imagine that she would never see Granda again.

How could that be?

She'd never again walk along the strand at Maidin Bay holding his hand. His hand was hard, she remembered, with calluses on his palms from digging in the potato field. She'd never sit in their house listening to his stories while the fire threw shadows across the whitewashed walls. So many stories he had told: about being a young man and fighting with the French against the English, about meeting her grandmother Bird at the fair in Drumatoole.

She thought of Sean then, and the ribbon he had pulled from her hair when she was eight.

Everyone was gone.

And Anna's cures, too.

In her mind she saw Anna bent over her table, her head raised in her little white cap, telling her, "If you want to cure, you have to know what will help and what won't."

She had knelt on Granda's bunk, Anna's seeds spilling on the coats, not knowing what would work, what wouldn't work.

She'd never try to cure anyone again. How terrible to think of a life without it, though. She had loved grinding the bits and pieces of flowers and leaves together; she had loved listening to Anna telling her about what to do, showing her how to soothe a cough, to bind a broken bone.

But maybe she had given Granda the wrong cure,

done the wrong thing. Maybe she knew nothing about cures that would help anyone.

*You've healed your foot*, Anna said in her mind.

It might have healed anyway.

*What about Eliza?*

Eliza was too tough to die.

Nory couldn't even cry. Her throat burned, and the back of her eyes. The wind had turned and she could feel her hair blowing against her face. If only she could sleep for a moment.

She heard someone leaning over her. "Miss."

She opened her eyes. It was Garvey, the steward. His thin face was red and she could see his hand trembling just a bit.

"I know you can heal," he said.

"That I cannot," she said.

"My friend is hurt," he told her. "He has been burned."

It ran through her mind quickly. *Buttermilk for sunburn. But for serious burns, one part beeswax to four parts mutton fat. Add camomile flowers. Keep the wound clean; keep it covered.*

But was it beeswax? Was it camomile? She didn't know anymore.

*You do*, Anna said.

Where would she even find beeswax or mutton fat? And she had thrown the camomile over the side of the ship. "I'm sorry," she told him. "It's no use."

Garvey looked desperate. "Do you know anyone then who will help?"

And then something else, something Anna had said

that Nory hadn't thought of since Granda died. *"Sometimes my cures work, and sometimes they don't. I wish I knew why."*

"He's in so much pain," Garvey said.

Hadn't Anna said something about that? *"Even if the cure doesn't work, it means something just to make the poor soul feel better."*

Patch was one of the children running. She could see that. A dangerous thing to do. One misstep on that slippery deck and he would slide, and suppose he went over the side of the ship? She caught her breath and pushed herself to her feet. "Patch," she called, but then she saw Eliza in back of him, watching.

"Are you coming?" Garvey asked.

"I was looking after my brother," she said.

*How can you not go?* Anna would say.

Eliza was playing a game with Patch. She had raised her dress over her ankles and was showing him how to do the steps of the basket game. Nory turned back to Garvey. "I have nothing to help your friend, but I will come anyway."

He nodded. "I haven't known what to do. I thank you, miss. I really do."

She followed him along the deck and down a long flight of steps. "Where are we going?"

"I'm hiding him. He's in a small area, a closet without light. The water oozes and barrels shift, but there is nowhere else."

A stowaway, then. She had heard of people like that, brave boys who sneaked aboard ships without money, without tickets.

"It is the cook's apprentice," Garvey said.

130

"Why . . . ?" she began, but there was no finishing. In front of her was darkness so deep she couldn't see Garvey, she couldn't see her own hand.

She reached out to hold on to his sleeve and followed him down the long passageway.

## TWENTY-TWO

### SEAN

He had been asleep a long time. But if he had slept that long, why did he ache so?

And then he remembered, or thought he remembered, the cook waiting outside the book man's cabin, waiting for him, marching him back to the galley without a word; the cook's hand heavy on his arm, his own heart beating, beating.

And then in the galley . . .

He didn't want to think about that. He wanted to think of Nory wearing a red ribbon in her hair, Nory at Patrick's Well on the cliff top, Nory singing, twirling, calling herself Queen Maeve.

Thirsty. So thirsty.

A hot day once in Maidin Bay. He and Nory had

leaned over Lord Cunningham's stream, drinking the icy water, splashing it on their faces.

If only he had a sip of water now. If only he could spill water over his head, over his arm.

In the galley the cook had hoisted a large pot of water from the stove. "Wastrel," he'd screamed. "Useless."

Sean had seen it coming, wondering how hot it was. He had raised his arms to cover his head, seeing Garvey jump out of the way. But it wasn't the pot of water the cook poured over the top of his head and over his shoulders that had scalded him. That water was hot but not boiling. But he couldn't catch his breath and he thought of the currach and the day he'd almost drowned in the green water of the sea.

He had fallen back against the stove. He heard the hissing as one arm hit the red-hot top; he heard the sound his own voice made. Then the cook was gone, and Garvey was pulling bits of his sleeve away from his skin.

And somehow he was in this place and he could hear the drip of the water and the *shush-shush* sound of the waves against the side of the boat.

If only he could drink some of the water.

He saw the lantern swinging over his head, just a point of light in the darkness, back and forth, back and forth.

"Ah, Nory," he whispered. "Let us go up to Patrick's Well."

She didn't answer, of course; she wasn't there. She

was home in Maidin Bay. But he heard the sound of crying then, a terrible crying that went on and on. Someone was leaning over him. The voice sounded like Nory's and the feel of the hand on his face was like hers, but he just couldn't open his eyes, and he slept again.

# TWENTY-THREE

## NORY

*What is the matter with you? There are things to be done.* That was what Anna would have said.

Nory drew a breath. There was so much to wonder at: how he had been burned, what he was doing on this ship and why she hadn't seen him, but most of all how she could save him.

The small candlelight flickered across his face and she knew she would save him. She thought it with the same fierceness she had felt when she had walked that long distance with Patch, each step burning and her foot leaking blood.

*Beeswax and mutton fat boiled together.*

Why should that work?

She thought of the beehive on the edge of Anna's field; she thought of the combs they had broken off to eat, hard and sweet. The wax would harden into the mutton fat. It would cover a wound to give it time to heal.

That made sense to her.

But there was no beeswax here, no mutton for fat. What else?

Garvey was watching her.

She made a roof of her hands over Sean's forehead and felt the fever like Granda's. "Do you have tallow for candles?" Without waiting for him to answer, she said, "Find some. And find fat."

"But the cook—"

"I don't care where you get it. Just do it and boil it, and stir it together and bring it to me."

She thought of Anna giving milk to Patch when she herself would have given anything for a sip of that warm froth on top. She thought of climbing the cliffs, wind howling, cupping eggs in her hands for all of them. She thought of that walk from Ballilee to the ship. And in front of her was Anna's face.

No more mixing of herbs when she didn't know what she was doing. No more throwing biscuits to birds that cared nothing for human food. She had to think, to use her head.

She took Garvey by the sleeve. "Boil fat with tallow and bring it to me," she said again, knowing that he would do it because if he didn't she would somehow do it herself.

She thought of Anna spreading her arms, her wrists thin as her blue sleeves fell back. "We're part of the earth," she had said, "but just as much part of the sea, the streams, the rivers. We need water to live, and the sick person needs it even more."

"And water," Nory said. "Not the water we've been drinking, but clear water, clean water."

"I can't—"

"Yes," she said, "you must," and turned away from him, pulling off her shawl to cover Sean with it. "You will be well, *a stór*," she whispered, hearing Garvey's footsteps going toward the door. She put her arm under Sean, holding him the way she had held Patch. She began to sing, the song she had sung when Maggie married Francey. She sang a song about the fair in Drumatoole, making up the words as she went along; she sang about the ribbon he had pulled out of her hair when she was a little girl. She felt her voice catch as she sang about his red hair and the year he had fallen into the sea.

Watching his face in that dim light, she knew he could hear some of it, and so she sang about a girl who was so glad she had found her friend, and how together they'd knock on her sister's door, his brother's door. They'd see his sister Mary, with her soft eyes.

And by that time Garvey was back with the water. "You may not think it is clean enough," he said. "The vat held wine before the trip, I think. But it is the best there is on this ship."

She reached for it, nodding her thanks.

"We are lucky," he said. "The cook has been drinking and sleeps at last, a deep sleep—for the first time in this voyage, I'm thinking."

Nory barely paid attention as he left again. She ripped her sleeve to the elbow and tore it into strips to soak in the water, first to wet Sean's lips and then to drip the water into his mouth.

She wet another strip and gently squeezed it over the burn, running the water over his arm, and did that until the water was gone.

And then Garvey was there and he had brought Patch with him. She watched Patch leaning over Sean, touching his forehead. "Where did you go, Sean Red?" he kept asking.

Garvey held wax and fat in a bowl, still warm from the heat of the stove, and held her shoulders to steady her from the motion of the ship. She stirred it, then covered Sean's arm with it from shoulder to wrist, watching it harden bit by bit, then wrapped a cloth over all of it, sitting back on her heels, trying to think if there was something else she could do.

"He will not die," she told Patch, and then said it again to Garvey.

"A burn like that . . . ," Garvey began.

She raised her hand, afraid that Sean would hear. "We will dance on the cliffs of Brooklyn."

"The cook will be looking for him," Garvey said slowly.

"And dance down Smith Street," she said, watching Sean's eyes move in back of his lids.

She didn't leave him, not that day, nor all the next. For hours Patch slept next to them rolled into a ball in Garvey's jacket.

The color came back into Sean's face, and once she saw that his eyes were open and he was looking at her as if he didn't believe she was there.

"I am real," she said.

Soon after that Garvey brought her tea, real tea, that colored the water a rich dark color. She had never tasted anything so wonderful, she thought, and he told her then that the cook had raged when he couldn't find Sean, and said he never wanted to set eyes on Sean's face again.

At last she realized that Sean was sleeping peacefully. She shared the rest of the tea with Patch, and a biscuit Garvey had brought, and then she leaned back against the bulkhead thinking she could sleep, really sleep. Maybe she would dream of the cliffs and Granda. If only he had been there, she would have been happier than she'd ever been. She thought too of her da and Celia in a ship ahead of them. Maybe by now it had found its way to Brooklyn: Da and Celia there, waiting with Maggie.

## TWENTY-FOUR

SEAN

It was a day he'd remember forever. Nory broke off pieces of the tough plaster and underneath was new skin, red and clean.

It was the day Garvey told them someone had seen green plants floating in the water, and a flock of small shorebirds had flown overhead. He told them too that it would be safe to go up to look. The cook had never once left the galley.

On the deck Sean watched as Patch begged Nory for a crumb of biscuit to throw from the side of the ship, "for the birds to help us with the rest of the journey." She broke off a piece, but Sean could see she didn't believe that story.

It was a story he had heard Mam tell, and he wondered if she was still alive. Nory had told him what happened, and it went through his mind that someday when he learned to write he would send a letter to Father Harte in Maidin Bay. He could almost see the priest, his soutane flapping as he climbed the hill to their house, and Mam there, listening to what he had written.

He felt a burning in his throat thinking of all this, and knew that Mam was probably gone like Nory's granda, but then he shook his head and thought of how hard he would work and the money he'd send. He told himself she would make the trip, but this time like the book man, in a cabin of her own.

Nory pulled at his sleeve. "Look, Sean Red."

Rising up out of the sea was the land, smoke from many fires rising gray above it, reminding him of coming home from fishing in the currach on a misty night to see the same charcoal look of the land.

A woman next to him pointed. "It's the port of New York," she said. "We've lasted through this whole terrible trip."

And Nory next to him: "That is Mrs. Casey," she said, "who tried to help Granda."

He turned. Next to the older woman was a young girl looking out at the sea. Her dark curls were cut close to her head, and Sean thought he had seen her before. In Maidin Bay? At the fair in Drumatoole? She wore a faded red ribbon around her neck. Someday he would buy another ribbon like that for Nory.

But he didn't have long to think about that. Garvey came running, breathless. "The captain sent orders," he said. "You must all sweep out the hold. Throw the old straw bedding overboard and anything that is not clean." He looked worried. "Wash yourselves because a doctor will be coming aboard."

"A doctor?" Nory said.

Garvey nodded. "You will be sent back to Ireland if he doesn't like the way you look."

Sean tried to help in the hold; he stayed as far away from the galley as he could, still anxious that the cook would see him. As he carried piles of straw up on deck he watched the land coming closer. Other ships were sailing not far from them, and people stood on those decks to throw things overboard. The sea was filled with straw, filthy bits of it floating on the waves, pieces of cloth and boxes bobbing along as well. "My coat," Patch said, pointing.

"How did we do that?" Nory said, turning to Sean. "How could we . . . ?"

"Never mind," Sean told them. "Everything will be new for us, and there will even be a coat for Patch by the time winter comes." He said it although he could hardly believe it, but somehow he would make it happen. He thought about reading too, and he knew he would make that happen as well.

They went back to the hold to wash the bunks and the planks under them with the muddy water they had left, and climbed the stairway one last time.

It seemed there was no room on deck for another person. Everyone had come up to watch as they angled for a place in the harbor. How long it would be, Sean wondered, before he reached Francey and Maggie in Brooklyn? Today? Tomorrow?

But right now he stood as straight as he could. The doctor was coming and he wanted to be sure he'd be one of the ones who reached the docks of New York.

BROOKLYN

## TWENTY-FIVE

### NORY

She had thought about this day so many times, but it wasn't at all the way she had pictured it. This flat place, boxes and papers littering the streets, horses clopping along ahead of them and in back of them. Houses crowded in on either side, all of them with windows, and rows of steps in front. And this was where they were going to live: a place that was a hundred times larger than Ballilee, a hundred times larger than Drumatoole.

She didn't see the diamonds in the streets the way she had thought she might, but it didn't make any difference. People stood in the streets talking to each other, laughing, people who didn't look hungry or dirty the way they had at home. People alive with full cheeks, and some with smiling faces.

Even the brightness of the day was surprising.

Brooklyn was hot; the sun beamed down on her head, an orange ball high above the houses, shining on the windows. Perspiration dampened her neck and her back, and next to her, Patch had drops on his small nose.

She loved this sun, and this heat. She loved the littered dirt roads that were bringing them to 416 Smith Street.

Turning to Sean, she saw the tears in his eyes. She reached out to put her hand on top of his. He must be thinking of his mother and his brothers Liam and Michael. Who knew where any of them were, or if he'd see them again?

"I'm all right, Nory," he said, turning his hand to hold hers. "The trip is almost over now."

She smiled. "And we're not even walking this last bit." How strange it was! They were driving in a carriage that had planks for seats, and a horse in front with a small plume tucked in its mane!

As they had put their feet on the gangplank that led to the dock, a girl had come toward them. "Where have you been?" she asked Sean, and, not waiting for an answer, gave him a book.

"The fox," he had said. "The wolf. I cannot take this."

She had looked impatient. "You must. That and a coin my father has sent for a carriage to take you where you are going. It is because you found me during the storm." She leaned forward. "You and I know it was a wonderful storm and I was safe." She tucked a coin into his hand and laughed before she darted away from them. Sean had stood there looking after her until

150

Garvey called to them. "Goodbye, your honors," he said. "Maybe we'll meet again."

"At 416 Smith Street," Sean called after him. "That's where we'll be." He ran to catch up.

Now in the carriage Nory put up her hand to touch the narrow ribbon around her neck. It had been there since she stood on the New York pier this morning, legs unsteady, on land for the first time in weeks but the rolling feeling of the ocean still with her. She had turned to see the rough wooden buildings along the pier, and people standing around them looking dazed to be there at last.

From in back of her had come a harsh voice: "I won't be seeing you again."

She had spun around and reached out to Eliza, to put her hands on those thin shoulders. "I wish you . . . ," she had said, trying to think of what it would be like not to see Eliza again. "I wish you everything good."

Eliza had bent her head with the soft curls that were beginning to grow again and untied the ribbon she wore around her neck. "This is for you, Nory Ryan."

"I can't take that," Nory had said, just as Sean had said it to the other girl a few moments earlier. Still she reached out to touch the softness of the faded ribbon.

Eliza smiled, her teeth dark. "For you, a remembrance."

Nory could see Sean wandering through the crowd of people just ahead of her now. She knew he was looking for her. "Oh, Eliza," she said. "I'll never forget you."

Eliza looped the ribbon around Nory's neck. "It belonged to a boy who shared his food with me. I tried to give it back to him, but he was gone." She bit at her bottom lip. "So many people on that terrible road."

Still feeling the ribbon against her throat, Nory raised her head to the sun as the carriage turned. Her bag shifted under her. Not much left in that bag, she thought—the wee cracked cup she'd keep forever to remind her of this long and bitter trip; Mam's wedding dress, wrinkled and stained on the bottom from the seawater; a few seeds and dried leaves scattered in the fabric, all that was left from Anna.

Never mind the stains. They'd air the dress on a pole outside. Never mind the leaves she had thrown overboard. She'd grow the few seeds that were left and find more somehow. She could see Anna in her head, her tiny white cap, her small hands. *Dear Anna, I won't forget what you've taught me.*

She could feel music in her head, songs she had sung in Ireland, bubbling up now, and she began to hum.

And then the carriage turned once more. She saw a row of stone houses in front of her, the sun glinting against the windows as the driver pointed with his crop. "This is where you're going," he said. "It's somewhere on this street."

She couldn't breathe. She felt as if something in her chest had become so large it was going to burst. She thought of Maggie the last day she had seen her, big Maggie with freckled face and hands. *"You're a great girl, Nory, a stór."*

The clopping of the horse's hooves slowed and the driver began to say the house numbers aloud.

"Look, Nory." Sean grasped her hand tightly in his and pointed with both of them.

A woman was coming down the steps with a baby in her arms, and a man leaned over them both, guiding them. "It's my own brother," Sean said. "Francey."

"Yes," Nory said, but she knew she wasn't making a sound. The carriage stopped as the man and woman reached the bottom step. And it was Sean who called out to Francey, Sean who said Maggie's name.

Patch climbed down from the carriage, but Nory felt as if she couldn't move, as if she would sit there forever. She watched Maggie, her face crumpling, holding the baby in one arm and Patch with the other hand, sinking down into the street. "Ah, Patch, Patcheen," Maggie said.

And then Nory was out of the carriage, dropping her bag, her legs with that strange feeling of still being on the ocean. She was close enough to see the part in Maggie's hair, the soft curls around her face, to hear Maggie sobbing as she rocked Patch and the baby together in the dusty street. And Francey, a step behind her, reaching out to Sean, both of them laughing and crying at the same time.

*Granda,* Nory thought. She went toward Maggie, still breathless. Tears blinded her as she ran her hands over her sister's thick hair, as she touched the small baby swaddled in a pink blanket, smiling at the blue eyes that were so much like Patch's, like Mam's.

Maggie struggled to her feet. "How long we've watched for you, waited for you."

She put her hand under Nory's cheek, turning her head so she faced the door. "Look now," she said.

And there was Da coming down the stairs, his arms out, the lines around his eyes deeper, his hair gray. He held his arms out to her, calling over his shoulder, "Celia, come!"

*All this time*, Nory thought as she went to meet him halfway. "We are here, Da," she managed to say, "here at last, *a stór.*"

In the late summer of 1845, people in Ireland awoke one morning to find their potato fields in ruin: blossoms gone, stalks bent, leaves covered with black spots. It was a devastating loss, for until that time, potatoes had been eaten by the poor for all their meals, anywhere from seven to fifteen pounds a day for each person.

The blight was caused by a fungus, *Phytophthora infestans*, and would return each year for the next several years. It was the worst hunger that Ireland had ever known. People starved to death or died from terrible diseases caused by lack of food.

Those who could get to the ships somehow, who could find the money for tickets, left Ireland, most of them to sail to America. My own great-grandparents were among them. They came from Galway, Meath, Tipperary, Longford, and Down, the Reillys to settle in

Brooklyn, New York, and the Tiernans, Cahills, and McClellans in New Jersey.

My ancestors were among two to three million people who left Ireland in the years after 1845. So many people! Anything that could sail was pressed into service: dirty ships, dangerous ships, old, rotting, and leaky, with scant supplies of food for the journey. The ships were so terrible they were called coffin ships. And coffins they were, often carrying the sick and dying. Some of the ships sank or were stranded on the rocks off the coast of North America.

It's hard to imagine those dark holds where people were packed together, seasick, homesick, and heartsick, trying to stay alive until they reached the shore. Many spoke only Gaelic; many couldn't read or write; some had only the clothes they wore.

In the early days when the first wave of Irish came, there was virtually no medical help, not on the ships, and not in the ports as they landed. They walked off the ships at the ports of America, hungry, weak, and penniless, to forge a new life for themselves.

Many of us are here because of their courage and determination to survive.

## ACKNOWLEDGMENTS

I owe a debt of gratitude to . . .

Wendy Lamb, angel editor, whose friendship I treasure as much as her expertise.

George Nicholson, my agent, who has been a part of my writing life from the beginning.

The supportive people at Random House . . . Judith Haut, Kenny Holcomb, Tamar Schwartz, Barbara Perris, Beverly Horowitz, Michelle Poploff, Terry Borzumato, Kathy Dunn, Adrienne Waintraub, Liz Rhynerson, Megan Fink, Alison Root, Kate Harris, and Susan Warga.

Dr. Eileen Reilly of New York University, whose willingness to meet with me in County Longford, knowledge of the period of which I was writing, suggestions for reading, and comments on the manuscript were enormously helpful.

The American Irish Historical Society, whose library was a quiet haven with warm and cheerful help just a step away.

Jimmy at Joyce House and the librarians at the National Library of Ireland in Dublin and at the Famine Museum,

Stokestown, who were more than patient in answering my questions and searching out material for me.

My grandmother Anne V. Maxwell, and Ella Frech, whose family stories made me want to know more about my heritage.

St. Jim, my husband, who has tramped the roads of Ireland with me all these years.

My children, who read, and comment, and read again.

And the six who are here to write for: Jimmy, Christine, Billy, Caitlin, Conor, and Patti.

BROOKLYN, 1979

## ABOUT THE AUTHOR

PATRICIA REILLY GIFF is the author of many beloved books for children, including the Kids of the Polk Street School books, the Friends and Amigos books, and the Polka Dot Private Eye books.

Several of her novels for older readers have been chosen as ALA Notable Books and ALA Best Books for Young Adults. They include *The Gift of the Pirate Queen; All the Way Home; Nory Ryan's Song*, a Society of Children's Book Writers and Illustrators Golden Kite Honor Book for Fiction; and the Newbery Honor Books *Lily's Crossing* and *Pictures of Hollis Woods*. *Lily's Crossing* was also chosen as a *Boston Globe–Horn Book* Honor Book.

Patricia Reilly Giff lives in Connecticut.

# BROOKLYN, 1875

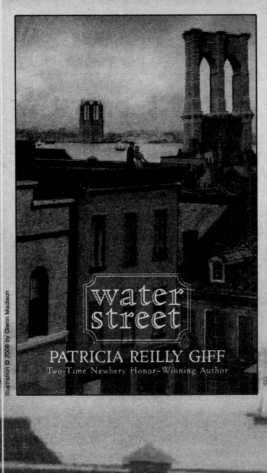

Illustration © 2006 by Glenn Madison

**water street**

PATRICIA REILLY GIFF
Two-Time Newbery Honor–Winning Author

The amazing bridge to Manhattan is underway. Just as this great time of change is coming for Brooklyn, so is this a great time of change for Bird. She wishes she could learn to be a healer like her mother, help her sister find love, and convince her brother to stop fighting in a street gang.

Most of all, Bird wishes for a friend.